How the Blessed Live

How the Blessed Live

Susannah M. Smith

Coach House Books

first edition, second printing

Published with the assistance of the Canada Council for the Arts and
the Ontario Arts Council

 Conseil des Arts
du Canada
 Canada Council
for the Arts

ONTARIO ARTS COUNCIL
CONSEIL DES ARTS DE L'ONTARIO

NATIONAL LIBRARY OF CANADA
CATALOGUING IN PUBLICATION DATA

Smith, Susannah M., 1967–
    How the blessed live

ISBN 1-55245-100-3

    I. Title.

PS8587.M593H68 2002   C811´.6   C2002-901618-5
PR9199.4.S54H68 2002

Isis and Osiris, having a mutual affection, loved each other in their
mother's womb before they were born ...
– E. A. Wallis Budge, *Egyptian Religion*

When the news reached the ears of Isis she was sore stricken, and
cut off a lock of her hair and put on mourning apparel. Knowing
well that the dead cannot rest till their bodies have been buried with
funereal rites, she set out to find the corpse of her husband.
– Lewis Spence, *Ancient Egyptian Myths and Legends*

I

Methods of Leaving the Body

BEYOND A WINDING RIBBON OF SAND, the water of English Bay supports mammoth bellies of cargo ships. The trees beside the seawall are still the deep green of summer. Behind the glass buildings of downtown, purple mountains are silhouetted against the sky.

She steps out of the cab and feels moisture on her skin, in her throat, curling her hair. Who says you can't remake yourself? Strange and desperate things happen to everyone. Her name is Lucy Gwendolyn Morgan and she is starting over, this minute.

She checks herself into a hotel overlooking the ocean. Out on the balcony, she leans against the wrought iron railing. In the distance, the dark body of Vancouver Island stretches across the horizon of water like a sleeping sea monster. She runs her hands unconsciously across her abdomen, her eyes drifting over the landscape. A flicker of fear behind her ribs. She turns back inside, starts humming to herself, something comforting, distracting, a Christmas carol about snow and a warm fire. She begins to unpack, taking her time hanging her clothes in the closet, carefully folding and stacking by colour in the bureau drawers. Balling up and throwing the long, striped witchy stockings in the wastebasket – no more magic spells for her.

When she gets down to the beach, low tide has exposed the densely barnacled rocks. Seagulls screech and soar in the wind. Her eyes scan the wave-patterned sand and she bends down, picking up shells and stones to fill her pockets.

After the sun drops beneath the horizon, she walks along Denman Street looking in store windows. At a corner grocer she buys a tin of sardines, a loaf of bread and some pomegranates. Back at the hotel, she empties her pockets, piling the shells and stones onto window ledges in her room. She lines the fruit up beside the shells to ripen. Little altars.

She floats in the bathtub, her legs crossed at the ankles, with the window open beside her, letting in the dark. Holding her nose, she slips her head beneath the surface, listening to the faraway pulse of the building's internal organs circulating heat, hot water, electricity. She bobs up and opens her eyes, inhales, rising higher in the water. Exhales. Sinking down to her eye corners. Inhale, rise up. Such high ceilings here. Exhale. Feeling the weight of gravity like a stone on her chest. Virginia Woolf. Ophelia. Blossoms. Splayed hair, a floating halo, death nimbus.

She pushes her arms against the sides of the tub, alternating, moving her body slowly back and forth. Her hair flows along with her, weeds in the tide. Crackle of wrist bones, small gold ring clinking against porcelain. How long does it take a drowned person to become waterlogged and sink? Do lost bodies move like this when they come to rest on the ocean floor?

A new day. Alone in a new city. The September sun is shining warm, and the air blowing in the window is fresh and salty on Lucy's tongue. She picks clothes in colours she doesn't usually wear together and puts them on. Outside, she buys a coffee and drinks it as she walks through the streets of the West End.

When she arrives at the art gallery, she opens the heavy doors, drops her coins in the box and walks through to the main foyer. White staircases curl up on either side of the rotunda, bathed in light from a domed window above. She makes her way to the top floor.

The walls are filled with paintings by Emily Carr. Deep, mysterious woods swirling with greens and browns. Tree branches and blue sky with so much life that they undulate against the flat canvasses. She goes to a glass case where some of the sketchbooks are displayed. She leans closer, taking in the ink drawings, the scribbled text. Then she smells cinnamon and senses someone standing to her left. Glancing quickly, Lucy sees a woman with big brown eyes and a mess of copper hair. The woman speaks first.

'Have you been to the second floor?'

'Not yet.'

'There's a forest down there.'

'A forest?'

'Yeah. An installation about trees. If you like Emily Carr – '

'I like your hair. It's a great colour.'

Lucy blurts it out. Unintentional. The woman smiles. Her teeth are bad but her lips are full and sensual. She has a lot of freckles. Something about her makes Lucy think of olives.

'I'm Cassy.'

She extends her hand. Her fingernails are curved and shining, growing out from a body that must be filled with moisture. There's dirt under her thumbnail and her hand feels cool.

'Lucy.'

Her eyes flicker up and down Lucy's body once before she withdraws her hand.

'Are you an art student?' she asks.

'No. Singer.'

'Where?'

'Mostly in the shower these days. And you, an actor?'

'Why?'

'You're not shy.'

'You don't seem too shy yourself.'

Lucy looks down at her boots, the hem of her skirt. This woman is making her say strange things.

'The Holy Circus is giving a performance tonight. Want to go?' Cassy asks.

'What is it?'

'Crazy-ass hocus-pocus theatre. Must be seen to be believed. If you want, I can pick you up.'

Cassy flashes her wide smile again. She's playing with a folded piece of her hair, flipping it back and forth with her fingers across her mouth. Near the back of her left earlobe is a tiny silver earring in the shape of a cat. Lucy is feeling hot and prickly, a wave of lava pushing its way up towards her skin.

They arrange to meet at the hotel at 7:30.

On her way from the gallery back to the hotel, Lucy stops and rests on a bench. She takes a folded piece of paper and a pen out of her bag and composes a list:

Catalytic: Variations on Desire
   aching behind my belly button
   wishing for relief
   craving a fancy
   I'd give my eye teeth for
   a sweet
   heart
   hunger and thirst
   (unsatisfied)
   to die for
   (a person who is dangerous)

She likes making lists. It smoothes out her insides.

∞

March 16, 1971

Gwendolyn (Wren) Morgan
b. February 6, 1944 d. March 11, 1971, age 27

There it is in black and white. True. Five days you've been gone now. Food has no taste. I carry you in the hollow of my stomach. I must write to you to feel human. I'll tell you everything so you can take part in the lives of our children. So you have eyes to see. Their lives and mine. So you never feel alone.

This is what I saw.

When it was time to move, the boy came first, one arm stretched out before him, reaching. The girl followed three minutes later, pushed forward on a tide of blood. Clotted and slick onto the sheet between your legs. It seemed to happen so quickly, all that awful blood. Then, somehow, suddenly, it was too late, and I was holding you. You looked into my eyes. And you were gone.

Fathomless.

I took the babies home, two flannel bundles. Quiet, like they knew crying wouldn't bring you back. Cinders whimpering, sniffing their new bodies, looking for you. I built a fire. The twins and me on the couch, Cinders lying on the warm linoleum beside the wood stove. All of us pulled down into uneasy sleep.

I never dreamed I would be doing this without you.

∞

She gets down to the lobby at 7:25 and Cassy is already there, sitting in one of the big armchairs, drinking and smoking a cigarette. Seeing Lucy, Cassy finishes the rest of her drink and stands up. She is wearing a black sweater and a pair of wine-coloured velvet pants. Her lipstick matches her pants and leaves a waxy crescent on the edge of the glass. She is a tightly coiled spring and moves quickly. Lucy takes a step back to give her space.

In the car, Cassy passes Lucy a crumpled piece of paper from her pocket. It's an address: 453 Richards Street.

She drives like she moves, in short bursts, with a kinetic intensity that is both alarming and attractive. Her head and hands constantly in motion. Lucy opens the window to let out the cigarette smoke, gripping the inside of the door with her right hand. Her head bobs back and forth as Cassy jerks her way into a parking spot, bumping the back of the car in front, and coming to a stop about a foot and a half from the curb.

She runs a hand through her hair, jangling a collection of multi-coloured glass bangles, and looks at Lucy, flashing a smile. 'I didn't say I was a good driver.'

They walk down a back alley and Cassy knocks on a warehouse door. It is opened by a woman wearing a peacock costume. The air is cool and damp inside the dimly lit entrance. They buy tickets and the peacock woman stamps their hands with a star that glows neon in the black light.

'You've only missed about fifteen minutes,' she says, waving them through with a viridescent arm.

Burning candles line the floor of the hallway. Lucy wanders into a room on the left. Cassy follows. A stage is set up at one end. They stand near the door with a few other people. Lucy feels Cassy near her elbow and there is the faint scent of her: cigarettes, cinnamon, brandy. Lucy shifts her weight from one foot to the other. Her arm brushes Cassy's breast. People stop talking as it gets dark and music starts to play.

A deep bass rhythm begins to fill the room like a heartbeat. Light gradually seeps into the darkness, and choral voices can be heard rising above the bass. As the light and music grow stronger, a tree floats down from the ceiling into the audience. A woman is perched in the tree wearing a sparkling white dress that clings to the curves of her body like fish scales. From her back spring two pale, opalescent blue wings that move slightly in the air. As the music fades out, she begins making birdcalls with her mouth.

Birds start flying in through two open doors and perch on her arms, the wires of her wings and the tree branches that surround her. There are sparrows, crows, finches, starlings, red-winged blackbirds, and they're all singing; the air full of chirping, cawing, trilling. Then the woman starts making loud peeping sounds that go higher and faster than the sounds of the birds. The air vibrates and begins to fill with butterflies, transforming the room into something plush and supple, alive with wings, colour and sound. After some time, the woman changes her tune, and as fast as they came, the birds and butterflies stream out through the open doors. The heavy, hypnotic music begins again as the shimmering bird-woman in her tree lifts up and out of the crowd.

Lucy can't speak. Cassy touches her arm and motions towards the hallway.

In the next room, a man is tied to a cross in front of the far wall. Censers billow fragrant smoke and stained-glass panels cast patches of coloured light onto the faces of the audience.

Lucy shoots Cassy a startled look.

'Is he okay?' she whispers.

Cassy nods quickly without saying anything.

The man hangs peacefully, his eyes half-closed, trance-like. He doesn't appear to be in pain and there are no nails, but he's got wounds in his hands, feet and side, which are dripping slowly, making small pools of blood on the cement floor. A recorded voice wraps the room in a cocoon of echoes. *You are free to approach and touch his wounds, take his blood into your hands and ask questions: Who is this man? Is he different from me? Is this a strange phenomenon? Can I believe it?*

Lucy moves forward and dips her finger in the blood by his left foot. It seems genuine. It's starting to congeal. Blood is dangerous these days. It's quite bold of him to bleed so flagrantly.

Cassy has gone on ahead. Lucy wanders towards a room that pours out electronic music, her body pulled towards the sound. Tall lightboxes line the walls. A naked woman with no hair moves in time to the music, doing a kind of slow underwater dance, snaking her body against the backdrop of light. She is sensual at the same time as she seems impossibly immaculate, having no superfluous flesh or hair to break her smooth surface.

When her eyes adjust, Lucy sees that the lightboxes are making the woman into an x-ray, her internal organs clearly visible through her skin, which forms a hazy white line around her edges. Lucy can see her liver, her intestines, her stomach. She can see her heart beating. This woman conducts light like metal conducts electricity.

She feels a hand on her shoulder. Cassy pulls her out of the room and into the corridor, where a man is standing.

'Lucy, this is Phineas Drake, the founder of the Circus.'

She extends the hand without blood on it.

'Hi, good to meet you.'

Something familiar about him causes her stomach to catch.

'I see you've experienced our stigmata man,' he says, glancing quickly at her fingers. 'How are you enjoying the show?' His head is cocked, a smile playing around his eyes.

Her mouth feels dry. She licks her lips.

'It's different.'

'She's a singer,' Cassy chimes in, leaning forward and squeezing Lucy's elbow. 'But she's too shy to tell you.'

Lucy feels herself blushing.

'What do you sing?'

When she answers, her tongue feels like wool in her mouth and her voice is an octave higher than usual.

'Oh, you know, standards, stuff I make up. Just odds and ends, really.'

He reaches into his jacket pocket and hands her his card.

'I'm auditioning new acts on Wednesday, if you're interested.'

The peacock woman comes up behind him, murmuring something into his ear.

'Please excuse me.'

He bows slightly and walks away.

Cassy leans over, her lips brushing Lucy's ear.

'I think he liked you. Not everyone gets a personal invitation.'

March 19, 1971

Wren,

Their names are as we planned: Levi if it was a boy, Lucy if it was a girl. Levi and Lucy. Our beautiful golden-haired twins.

After the funeral I wanted only to lie down and sleep. Being there was exhausting – seeing your parents, my mother and sister, all our university friends. Could barely talk to anyone. Going through the motions.

That damn poem we used to sing has been circling round my head now for three days – the Christina Rossetti one. Remember?

> *'Ferry me across the water,*
> *Do, boatman, do.'*
> *'If you've a penny in your purse*
> *I'll ferry you.'*

Now it's part of me, like a deadhead on the lake, knocking up against the shore with each wave. Useless without you.

How could you leave me with all of this? My hands so full and so empty.

The day of her audition, Lucy sleeps in late, wakes up ravenous and orders room service. When the food arrives – French toast with butter, maple syrup and strawberries, scrambled eggs, a pot of tea, grapefruit juice – she suddenly feels nauseous and loses her appetite. All she can manage is the tea. She runs a bath, pouring bubbles under the tap, making a mountain of suds. She looks at herself standing naked in front of the bathroom mirror. Her body feels unfamiliar, as if it belongs to someone else. She is tired. Her breasts are swollen and hurt with the slightest touch or movement. A seed of panic sprouts in her. *What if I billow up like a huge balloon? What if I start growing and just don't stop?* She wishes that this were Wonderland, that there were a little bottle or cake to shrink her into a smaller size in case she gets too big. She climbs in the tub and leans back, sipping the clear tea, comforted by the weightless suspension she feels. Amniotic.

20

She had that sense of certainty when Phineas mentioned the auditions. Like those times when she's showering, eyes closed, head streaming with the wet rush of hot water, and she can feel the vast oiled machine of the cosmos clicking behind her skull. A glimpse of events usually hidden from view – the entire mechanism in sync, one gear grooved to fit into the next. Singing with perfection.

She prepares, deciding to wear the pink skirt with silver flowers stitched onto the hemline. She has chopped her hair off and dyed it a deep bluish black, a mess of twirled licorice. Midnight Sky, the box said. A new colour, a new you. Addictive.

She puts on pale blue eyeshadow and the lipstick with peppermint oil that makes her lips tingle. A close-fitting black shirt and she's ready to go.

The place is distinguishable only by a small turquoise bird painted above the door handle. She climbs the steep stairs slowly, taking deep breaths to collect herself, sniffing quickly under each arm. Her mind skitters back to her audition at the Royal Conservatory in the spring. How she was sweating then, trying to maintain her composure, smiling at the jury before opening her mouth to sing.

She looks up just as a woman wearing a feather boa brushes past on her way down. A couple of brilliant blue feathers are swept up in the air behind her as she disappears out the door.

At the top of the stairs, the room is dark and quiet. Plush burgundy chairs and violet glass. Lucy stands for a moment listening to her own breathing. Calm. Her clothes cling damply to her skin. She licks her lips. Thirsty. A mild wave of nausea grips her and then passes. She swallows, her throat dry.

'Yes, please come in.' A man's voice somewhere in the darkness.

She moves towards the voice like a swimmer, arms pushing through humid air. Then he appears before her, seated at a round table beside a dance floor.

He pours her a glass of water from a pitcher in front of him and motions for her to sit down.

'Thank you.' She drinks half the water from the glass, keeping her eyes on him.

'I'm Lucy. We met the other – '

'I remember.' He refills her glass, smiles and leans back in his chair. He is wearing a white cotton shirt, open at the neck. His dark hair falls in loose curls around his face. His hands are graceful, with long fingers. She can imagine him playing an instrument. She wonders where he is from, how old he is. She feels conspicuously pink and blue and glittering.

'To be honest, Mr Drake, I'm not sure why I'm here. I enjoyed your Circus, but I'm not like any of those people. I'm not really a professional singer yet. I mean, I got a scholarship to the Conservatory but I had to defer until next year, so … I'm just starting out.'

Phineas looks at her as if he's seeing something just beyond her head. She pulls herself up so she's sitting straight and meets his gaze. She can't decide if it's pleasant or unnerving. She hopes her voice doesn't break.

'And yet you came here today. So why don't you try singing something for me and we'll go from there.'

She notices that he is playing with a small aqua-coloured bird like the one on the door, rolling it back and forth across his palm. It looks hard, like it's made of some kind of stone or mineral. She's feeling hungry. The bird looks good enough to eat. She wants to lick it.

'Anything?'

'Whatever you want.' His voice is smooth, gentle.

She stands up and moves towards the middle of the dance floor. Her black shoes make a good clip-clap sound as she walks. She turns her back to him and closes her eyes. Taking a deep breath, she begins quietly, remembering how Judy sang it in the movie, yearning, her face young and fresh, with those big eyes and ruby lips.

Somewhere over the rainbow, way up high,
There's a land that I heard of once in a lullaby,
Somewhere over the rainbow, skies are blue,
And the dreams that you dare to dream really do come true.

Her voice is faint, barely more than a whisper. She hopes that he can hear her.

Someday I'll wish upon a star
And wake up where the clouds are far behind me,
Where troubles melt like lemon drops,
Away above the chimney tops, that's where you'll find me.

She is gaining strength now. Feeling something like elation building behind her ribs.

Somewhere over the rainbow, skies are blue,
And the dreams that you dare to dream really do come true,
If happy little bluebirds fly
Above the rainbow, why oh why can't I?

She finishes, feeling taller, wider, sweat beading on her forehead. She wipes her face with the back of her hand and turns around. His expression is unguarded, hands folded in his lap. She smiles as she approaches the table, and so does he, his teeth a white puncture glowing in the murk of the room.

'Thank you. That was lovely.'

She isn't sure if he is serious or not. She looks down at her fingers. She did a good job of applying her nail polish this morning. It is perfect and shimmering and doesn't touch any of her cuticles.

'I need to hire a personal assistant. Would that interest you?' he asks, his voice pulling her back.

'I know it was just a standard song –'

'The song was fine, Lucy. Don't get me wrong, I think we could use you in the Circus, but right now, I really need an assistant. Our shows for this year are finished, and I'm preparing for our spring tour. Paperwork, interviews, promotion, that kind of thing. You could start right away.'

She pauses, realizing that her nervousness has disappeared.

'I'll need some time to think about it.'

'Of course. Call me when you've decided.'

She stands up to go and they shake hands. His grip is warm and firm.

She looks in his eyes; they're dark brown, deep-set. 'Is it really happening, what goes on in those rooms, or is it done with a lot of gizmos?' she asks him.

He nods, pushing his hair behind his ears and walking with her towards the back of the room where she came in. 'Well, I'm not the great Oz, if that's what you mean, but it's an understandable question. They are things we aren't used to seeing every day. My question for people who come to see the Circus is whether being unable to explain something means that it can't exist. Science can explain how a fetus develops inside a woman's uterus, but it still can't understand the innate ordering of information, the miracle of cellular intelligence.'

She realizes she is looking at him with her mouth agape and snaps it shut. He starts talking again before she can reply.

'I've come to believe that there are many possible ways of being human.' He smiles and shakes her hand again before turning around and disappearing back into the dim room, leaving her alone at the top of the stairs.

'See you soon,' she hears him call out.

She makes her way down to the door. Out on the street she feels rain on her head and lifts her face to the heavy dusk of the sky.

March 23, 1971

Wren,

What is left is here beside me in a canister. A few ashes. Your body.

There will be no burial and slow decomposition. You will not become worms. I know this is the way you would have wanted it – the clean sweep of fire, pure and final. Though we never spoke of such things.

I will carry you outside after daybreak. Into your birds, your sun on my back and face, into your wind. I will take you up onto the hill near the plum trees, and I will free you to the elements there. You will live on this land and around this house forever. You will always be a part of this place.

In Kitto on Granville Street it's starting to get busy with early dinner customers. Japanese pop music blares above the buzz of conversations. Steam fogs the windows, transforming the restaurant into a cozy bubble of happiness. Lucy orders her new favourite things: green tea, vegetable tempura, steamed rice and a salmon roll. The perfect meal to fill her up and keep her light. Just the right amount of food – satisfying without giving her that stretched-out feeling. A tiny laxative every other day to keep the whole thing moving, and she is a pipeline, narrow and lean.

She is letting herself be absorbed here, becoming Asian from the inside out. Transforming through the powers of daikon radish, ginger, green tea, seaweed and rice. Loving the way that sushi looks like cells. Seaweed cell wall, rice protoplasm, fish and vegetable nucleus. Like eating a miniature version of life itself.

She imagines her new Japanese self: beautiful, with a musical laugh and a sweet smile. Flawless skin. Straight black hair. No unnecessary body fat. She will stay up late eating noodles, drinking coffee and watching movies with her friends, laughing. She will travel all over the world taking pictures. Happy all the time.

She walks to Chinatown, giving herself over to the exotic, basking in the frenzy of stimuli. Weeping carcasses of meat in windows. Salted turnip, two bags for ninety-nine cents. Tea in tins: gunpowder, jasmine, chrysanthemum, Oolong, Pu-erh. Bags of fortune cookies. Heaps of bok choy, knobby jackfruit, flattened chicken legs, pork hearts, lychee nuts, spiky-haired rambutan. Shelves of clear plastic boxes containing preserved plum, mango and pineapple. Everything salted and shrivelled, with a shelf life extending into eternity. She allows herself to be carried along, unnoticed in the warm press of bodies and the hubbub of voices. It's like she's in another country, among friends, but safely anonymous. Entirely at home in the sea of people.

Back at the hotel, suddenly exhausted, she sleeps and dreams of dogs. When Cinders disappeared, her father said she had run away with the wolves, but Lucy never believed him. In these dreams, Cinders is back. Lucy holds the dog's head in her lap while Cinders licks her hands. She strokes the floppy velvet ears with her fingers, pressing her cheek against them. Nothing in the world as soft as this.

She wakes and catches herself thinking of Cassy. Imagines being curled up in her arms, Cassy's hair falling in an amber curtain between them and the world. Finding a kind of shelter in the glow of her fire.

⁂

April 10, 1971

Wren,

Learning how to be both a mother and father. So little time to write, but you mustn't think I've forgotten you. Sometimes it feels like you're giving me the energy to get up in the morning. Animating my limbs, taking care of these babies through me. Their bodies held together by your cells.

I reduced my shifts on the ferry to thirty hours a week, at least until the twins are old enough to go to school. Three ten-hour days, and I've hired the eldest McGregor girl to help out. You always liked her, and I know she's responsible. It's really only a few hours out of the week. I'll manage.

Lucy says yes to his offer.

Phineas Drake's office is in his house, which faces out towards the Georgia Strait and the green bulb of Stanley Park.

'We live right across the water from each other. I'm at the Hotel Sylvia,' she says, pointing to the opposite shore.

He squints along the line of her finger and raises his eyebrows. 'Expensive.'

'I have some money from my mom,' she answers without looking at him.

He cocks his head and looks at her, bringing his lips together in a line. Walking over to his desk, he finds a scrap of paper, writes a phone number on it and hands it to her.

'Call my friend Theo. He manages a couple of buildings in the West End. Tell him I gave you his number, that you're working for me. He'll find you something more affordable.'

The apartment is on the eleventh floor and faces south, one block from the ocean and two blocks from Stanley Park. Huge windows and a sliding glass door make up the entire south wall. Outside, seagulls soar and cry in the air. All around, people are in similar rooms, bees inhabiting their hives. A curious way to live, Lucy thinks.

There is a bed and a couch that look like they have never been used. The kitchen has a set of dishes and a few pots and pans. She unpacks her clothes and hangs them in the closet, then lines up her rocks and shells on the bedroom window ledge.

She goes out and buys flannel sheets and a quilt. Some groceries. A few candles. Bubble bath.

Back in the apartment, she leans against the closed door, sets the grocery bags down and looks around. Feels a lump in her throat, and sits down on the couch. Then, as quickly as it came, the threat of tears passes. She stands up. Puts the food away in the fridge. Relieved.

Later, in bed, her skin feels smooth against the sheets. She lies on her back, eyes closed, remembering the pillows of Cassy's lips, the heat of standing next to her. She runs her hands slowly over her body. Lightly over her tender breasts, down over her ribs, across the plane of her stomach, into the warmth between her thighs. She is water, moving back and forth, in and out, coming in waves.

After spending most of the next day wrapped in thick sleep, clotted with strange dreams she can't quite remember, Lucy feels restless and goes out walking at sundown.

She stops at a café to rest. A man sitting at the window reads a book, scribbling intently in the margins. She wishes for a book like that. One that she could carry with her, writing notes in the white spaces, turning down the corners of the best pages. One that would offer itself up to her, making sense of things. She would turn to any page and find the answers to her questions. A sort of bible.

At night, she finds an old copy of *National Geographic* in a closet. She rips out pictures of volcanoes and tapes them to the walls of the apartment. She thinks about fire, about the fact that right now, at this moment, in different parts of the world, there are earthquakes happening. And because of the earthquakes, volcanoes are erupting, producing hot, choking clouds of ash that eclipse the sun. Somewhere, right now, volcanologists are wearing heatproof suits and helmets while they walk next to red-hot rivers of lava. Walking through fire, like science fiction, like magic.

Lying on the bed, unable to sleep, she wishes for apple pie, warm and cinnamony, with cheese, and a milky cup of hot chocolate. She wishes for a woman to hold her, to sing her a lullaby. A woman who loves her, with hips, thighs, breasts, warm hands and breath a comfort to her skin. The fullness of her body, solid and real.

Tools of the Trade:
invisibility ring
flying carpet
golden belt
seven-league boots
protection stone
well for throwing enemies down
knowing cap
wishbone

∽

August 14, 1971

Wren,

Saturday. A day off. The twins down for a nap. It's one of those summer days. Overcast and thick with humidity. I'm sitting by the open window. Dampness settling on my legs and ankles. Crows fussing in the trees outside, their throat-voices abrasive. A blue jay, its piercing cry soothing in comparison. Now, a fine mist coming down. Can't really call it rain.

Your eyes misted over. You were sitting across from me at this very table. The mist turned to tears as you lay your head down on your arms and sobbed. I reached over and rested my hands on your shoulders while they shook. A minute or two passed before you lifted your head and looked at me. You took both my hands in yours.

'I think it's time, Daniel.'

'For what?' I asked, though I think I knew.

'I want to have a baby. I don't want to wait any longer.'

I paused before replying. Choosing my words carefully. The voice of reason.

'You're sure? It'll change everything. Our routines. Quiet. Freedom. Our lives will never be the same.'

'So, you don't want to?'

'No, it's not that. I just want to be realistic …'

'I've thought about it a lot. I think maybe we could use a change in our house, don't you? A little noise, a little chaos. Are you ready?'

'Of course I'm ready. We've always said we wanted a family together, it was just a matter of when. If you're ready, then I am.'

Your eyes filled with tears again. I stood up and came around to your side of the table, sliding onto the bench beside you. I put my face in close to yours.

'Did you already take your pill today?'

You laughed, wiping tears from your cheeks.

'No, not yet.'

'Don't,' I whispered in your ear.

I put one arm under your legs and one arm across your shoulders, lifted you up and carried you across the living room towards the couch.

'We must begin this project immediately,' I said, setting you down and lowering myself beside you.

∞

Sometimes she still can't believe she's here. That, at any time, she can board the sea-bus and glide across the channel to the north shore. Transported by water to the sun-glittering buildings against their unreal backdrop of mountains. Where she can walk in the dripping trees, surrounded on all sides by ferns, moss draped from branches, life pushing out and out and out. This must be the promised land, she thinks, an enchanted fairy world, where the green heart is still intact.

Almost every day, she walks beside the ocean, letting the air and water find a home in her skin. On the seawall, she sometimes sees women pushing baby carriages. She looks at them, feeling the churn in her stomach. *She's a mother.* Looks at the faces of the babies. They make her think of aliens. Mysterious pod people with big bald heads. Their eyes blinking open and closed, moving slowly under moist glossy lids, taking everything in. Practically transparent pink fingers and toes. Vulnerable, yet unnerving. Their wide-eyed silence, hiding the fact that they know things. That they've got the goods and they're not talking.

∞

December 7, 1971

Wren,

Some days, the finest thing is the steady sound of Cinders's teeth crunching food, the sloppy lapping of water from her plastic dish. Small certainties. A kind of glue, holding me together.

Despite the help I'm getting, between the babies and work, I am consumed.

There are so many moments – on the boat during crossings, while the twins are sleeping – when I fall back into memories.

How we both loved hot summer afternoons that turned stormy. The time when the sky went black in minutes, wind whipping up the trees, sending ripe apples falling onto the roof of the woodshed with a dull thud. 'It's an apple storm,' you said. 'It's raining apples.' They fell through the late summer, littering the yard, baking brown and syrupy in the sun, drawing bees with the sweet smell of fermentation. We sat on the back porch while it rained, watching the lightning, drawing closer at the loud claps of thunder, waiting until it passed over. Afterwards, the air was full of electricity and the smell of damp earth. We had all the time in the world.

So why did you leave early? Didn't we have an agreement to stay in this together to the end? Is any of this getting through to where you are? Wherever that is.

It is raining. Lucy turns on the gas fireplace and stretches out on her stomach across the floor with a pen and some paper. Letting her hand doodle words and shapes. Getting her fingers black with ink. Smudging the words with spit on her finger. Humming, singing the words as she writes.

The phone rings. It's Cassy.

'Hey, stranger, you trying to avoid me? I called the hotel but you'd already left.'

A vein of fear spikes through her.

'Oh my god, I'm so sorry – I totally forgot.'

Lucy hears herself tell the lie easily.

'It's okay, I called Phineas Drake and he gave me your new number.'

'I feel like an idiot … '

'Forget it. You busy? Want to go out for a while?'

They arrange to meet downstairs in half an hour.

Lucy changes quickly, pulling on clothes that make her feel sexy. A low-cut crimson shirt without a bra, a black satin skirt with Chinese embroidery, green stockings, her Doc Marten boots, a sparkly ring, lipstick. She rubs her lips together, spreading the colour just over the edges, giving more fullness, as though she's been kissing. She doesn't bother washing her ink-stained hands.

Waiting downstairs, she smokes a cigarette from the package she keeps for nervous situations, ignoring the No Smoking sign, wishing she had a long cigarette holder. When Cassy comes bursting through the door, she is already lightheaded from the nicotine.

Lucy floats beside her as they walk along the seawall under a transparent umbrella, a portable plastic skylight. Cassy reminds her of a jester, stepping lightly, a hop to her gait, as if she is going to jump up and twirl around in the air, jangling silver bells on a pointed cap. Her hair is swept into a messy red knot that is more falling out than staying in. It looks slippery. Lucy's hand goes up to her own hair, short and stiff from the dye, playing with it, stirring it into knots.

Lucy's feet are wet. 'Let's head back,' she says.

'I'll buy us a drink,' Cassy replies, grabbing Lucy's hand. They turn around and start running together, both of them gulping mouthfuls of moist, cedar-flavoured air. Back on Davie Street, Cassy pulls her into a liquor store where she buys a bottle of brandy.

In the apartment, Cassy's pants and Lucy's tights hang over the back of a chair near the fireplace. Cassy has a blanket wrapped around her legs and is wearing a pair of Lucy's socks. Lucy has changed into a dry skirt that touches the ground when she walks. The brandy is making her stomach warm, radiating heat through her body.

'Mind if I smoke?' Cassy asks.

'I'll have one, too,' Lucy tells her.

Cassy pulls a pack of cigarettes from her bag on the floor beside her. There is the flicking sound as she offers Lucy a light. The first drag, most delicious, smoke mixing with brandy, hot on the way down.

'I'm pregnant, you know,' Lucy tells her. A lump rising in her throat. The new words hanging in the air.

Cassy glances down at her abdomen. 'No.'

'Yeah, really. Just a few weeks, though.'

'You're going to have it?'

'Looks that way.'

'Hmmm. Braver than me.'

Cassy toasts her feet in front of the fireplace.

Lucy looks down into her drink, swirling the amber liquid around in slow circles. When she looks up, Cassy is staring intently at her.

'So, are you acting in a play right now?' Lucy asks her, deflecting her eyes.

Cassy curls her hands into claws and screws up her face:

Round about the cauldron go; in the poison'd entrails throw. For a charm of powerful trouble, like a hell-broth boil and bubble.

'Let me guess: *Macbeth*.'

'Someone knows her Shakespeare.'

Lucy points to Cassy's open bag on the floor, where a tattered copy of the play is visible.

'Oh, there I go, spilling all my secrets.'

'Where's it showing?'

'Outside at Vanier Park. There's a dress rehearsal tomorrow at eight if you want to come.'

'Okay?'

Lucy stretches her legs out beside Cassy's and leans her head back on the couch. She can hear her breathing. Cassy turns her head to Lucy, their faces a couple of feet apart.

'I should get going. I've got to work,' Cassy says.

'Where's that?'

'Delilah's. I'm a waitress – every actor's second career of choice.'

Lucy feels drunk. They stand, and she tries not to look at Cassy's lips, at the curve of her foot when she slips on her shoe. Cassy leans over and gives her a hug. And then, somehow, they're kissing. Cassy cupping Lucy's head in her hands, snaking fingers through her hair.

She moves Lucy up against the wall, their tongues warm and slow, chests pressed together. Lucy feels Cassy's hand drift under her shirt, smoky and smooth, finding one breast, then the other, fingers moving lightly across her nipples. Cassy lifts her own shirt and guides Lucy's head down to her breast. Lucy closes her eyes, then feels Cassy's other hand rubbing quickly and rhythmically between her own thighs. She tenses and shudders before gently pushing Lucy away and glancing at her watch.

'Oh my god, now I really do have to go', she says, standing up, straightening her clothes, and tying her hair back up.

'Okay?'

The world seems hazy and Lucy can't think of anything else to say. Cassy gives her a quick kiss on the mouth and turns to leave. 'Call me,' she says. When she turns her head, Lucy sees the silver cat glint once from Cassy's ear, and then she is gone, disappearing down the hallway.

Lucy closes the door, leaning against it for a minute. Exhausted, she lies down on the couch, and within seconds, she is asleep.

＄

Phineas thinks he's found a new act for the Circus and wants Lucy's opinion. Sure, she says, so off they go to a bank downtown.

'Why a bank?' she asks him.

'That's where she wanted to be. Like all that money, I suppose, tucked away for later.'

'Who?'

'The woman who sleeps under water,' he answers. 'Not many people know she's here, just a few of the bank employees.'

He takes her into a back corner past a column and some tall plants. They walk down a hallway and into an empty office where the blinds are drawn. Lying in a clear, lidless glass box filled with water and strewn with orange blossoms, is a woman. She appears thin and fragile, her face suspended just above the surface of the water, short blonde hair floating out around her head.

'She looks good for a woman who's well into her eighties, doesn't she? Well-preserved,' Phineas whispers.

Lucy stares. The woman looks like she is maybe thirty-five years old. As they stand there, she stirs occasionally, repositioning herself in the water, but keeps her eyes closed. Under the thin white dress she has on, Lucy can see her tiny ribcage rise and fall almost imperceptibly with each breath.

'She has to be treated very carefully – only looked at, not touched or disturbed by noise or voices louder than whispers. She needs peace and quiet, so she can rest and save herself for the future,' Phineas tells her.

When he asks Lucy what she thinks, she is speechless for a minute. When she finds her voice, her tongue is thick and unfamiliar. 'She's so perfect. But what about her privacy?'

Phineas nods slowly, keeping his eyes on the floating woman as he speaks in a low voice. 'Her need for secrecy may be strong, but I'll wager that her vanity is stronger. The Circus would give her a way to be protected yet seen, in the world yet separate from it. I think it could be the ideal place for her.'

At night, alone in the apartment, the floating woman is taking up space in Lucy, hanging around like a fog, the way an air of sickness permeates a room. Lucy wonders what goes on inside her. *What does she do while she's lying there? Sleep? Plan? She has no life. Maybe Phineas is right. The Circus is perfect for a weirdo like her.*

> *Freaky Freaks:*
> *A leg growing out of your head*
> *Green skin*
> *A fish tail and gills*
> *Six fingers on your left hand*
> *One leg shorter than the other*
> *Deaf in one ear*
> *Blind in one eye*
> *One lung*
> *Two hearts*
> *No visible handicaps, limping on the inside*
> *A smaller version of yourself lodged in your torso, its head buried next to your spleen*
> *Pregnant with a monster*

March 19, 1972

Wren,

Finally having the courage to go through some of your things, to face them. When I opened the bottom drawer of your bureau it was filled with the silky seeds of exploded milkweed pods. You must have collected them when they were green and hidden them away.

It's like you sent me a letter and I'm only getting it now.

I didn't have it in me to clean them up. I left them there, the drawer open a crack. Every once in a while a seed floats past in the house. Your presence moving through a room.

Sometimes you exhaust me.

The evening is clear and cool. Behind the tent, the mountains are dark sentinels against a pink sky. Lucy finds a seat near the stage and pulls her sweater close around her.

The three witches dance in a circle, whirling their awful black rags, shaking their naked breasts, showing their teeth. Cassy's eyes are wide and crazed as she cackles and chants:

> *Fillet of a fenny snake,*
> *In the cauldron boil and bake;*
> *Eye of newt and toe of frog,*
> *Wool of bat and tongue of dog,*
> *Adder's fork and blind-worm's sting,*
> *Lizard's leg and owlet's wing …*

She stomps, her feet appearing and disappearing from beneath the edge of her skirt. The material is thin, sepulchral, flowing around her like vapour. Through it Lucy can see the darker outline of her underwear, a thin triangle of cloth, a thong that disappears between her buttocks. She's overdramatizing, but Lucy loves watching her – the skin near her throat rising and falling as she speaks, her chest glistening with a fine shimmer of sweat. Lucy shifts in her chair.

She wants to lay her head there again. To be wrapped in the layers of Cassy's dress. She wants to be closer than this.

That night she tosses and turns, witches dancing behind her eyes, bodies contorted, huddled over their pot. Visited by Hecate and singing a black song to bring their potion to life. Lucy sees Cassy's face flashing through her red hair. Her shaking breasts. The sublime curve of her foot.

> Hecate:
> *(Invoked by those who set out on journeys)*
> *Queen of witches, magic, the ghostworld*
> *Goddess of dark places, moonless nights and crossroads*
> *Guide to the underworld*
> *Greek for 'the distant one'*

The next day, Lucy thinks she will surprise Cassy by visiting the restaurant where she works. Maybe have a little something to eat, a glass of wine. Maybe see her again when she finishes her shift.

'Cassy who?' the guy at the door says.

She tries to remember her last name from the program notes.

'Harding. Cassandra Harding. A bit taller than me. Slim, with shoulder-length red hair.'

'Doesn't ring a bell.'

'Are you sure? She's an actress, kind of hyper, smokes a lot?'

'Nope, sorry. I've been working here for over a year now, and there hasn't been a single redhead. You're sure you came to the right place?'

She nods and asks to use the bathroom. Looking at herself in the mirror, she takes deep breaths to calm the thread of anger that is floating behind her ribs. Her face looks a bit tired, pale. As she leaves, a sign on the paper towel dispenser catches her eye.

'Warning: Drinking spirits during your pregnancy can harm the baby.'

She walks for more than an hour on her way home, clearing her mind in the night air. She chides herself: *There is nowhere to go with this wanting. Can't love a liar. Can't love a girl. Can't be trusted. If I could say a spell, I'd make you disappear.*

Lucy's resolve falls apart the moment she hears Cassy's voice on the phone in the morning.

They sit on a patio overlooking the water. It is cool and sunny. Beside them, the masts of sailboats clink in the breeze.

'How was work last night?' Lucy asks her. 'Was it busy?'

'A madhouse,' Cassy answers.

Lucy can't help but look at her mouth, the glint of teeth behind her lips.

'I stopped by to see you last night but the guy at the front said you weren't there.'

'You went to the restaurant?'

Cassy looks angry, her eyes narrowed, two pink spots appearing on her cheeks.

'Yeah, I was walking by and wanted to see you, but the guy at the front said you didn't work there. But it's not a big deal. We all need our secrets, right?' Lucy tries to smile.

Cassy lowers her eyes, lifting her glass up and down, leaving a trail of water rings on the plastic tablecloth.

'Yeah, well, I don't like people following me around.' Her voice is quieter now.

'Sorry, I just wanted to see you, that's all.'

She's gathering up her things.

'Cassy, I said it doesn't matter. I don't care that you don't work there.' Lucy reaches out to touch her hand and Cassy brushes her away.

'I've got to go.'

'Cassy, I think you're overreacting.' She pauses. 'What about the other day?'

Lucy's voice is practically a whisper now. She feels a tide of panic rising. She has to make her stay. Cassy's eyes flash up briefly.

'Look, the other day never happened. I have a boyfriend. I'm not into this woman-love shit. I've got to go.'

She slams some money down on the table.

A door in Lucy closes.

'I'm sorry,' she says, but Cassy's back is already turned. She strides away, the sun falling into her hair, lighting it up. Lucy watches until she disappears in the distance. She doesn't go after her. She stays sitting at the table in the sun, as if nothing has happened. Swallowing back a wave of nausea. Remembering what she learned in voice lessons, regulating the breath to relax tension. Pushing down her hunger. When someone wants to leave, there's no point in trying to stop her.

∞

October 22, 1973

Wren,

On the boat today, face into the wind, water spray in the air. I watched the churn of the propeller, the trail the boat made, deep green crested with white froth. I watched the island and the mainland approach and recede, the ferry a pebble bouncing back and forth between two shores. My hands directing traffic, independent of my brain. Only the twins and you keeping me in this world.

Last night, I thought I heard footsteps in the hall, floorboards creaking, walls knocking. I pushed up out of sleep, groggy. Still dreaming,

I swam in a moment of half-consciousness, reached out across the bed, forgetting that you were gone. Holding off the realization of the present as long as I could, until it crashed against me, a cold wave – that I will not hear your steps echoing down that hallway again. I will not draw the heat of your body close to mine when you return to bed, after getting up to go to the bathroom as you always did partway through the night.

I lay awake, engulfed by darkness. The house continued to make its night noises. I reminded myself of the science of heat and cold, the expansion and contraction of wood with moisture, the sound a brick makes when it cracks. I reminded myself that you cannot be alive in me and a phantom simultaneously. That I carry you in my body, so you cannot wander outside of it. This is not an orchestra of ghosts, I told myself.

When I fell asleep, my dreams were of being repeatedly thrashed by waves against the sharp rocks on the south side of the island. When I looked at them, it was your face I saw.

∽

Lucy is sorting through photos. Phineas wants her to make a poster for the Circus. He tells her it's easy, to just take her time. She says she hopes he has a lot of time, that she's never used a computer. 'Don't worry,' he replies. 'Time is a fluid concept and can be stretched. I have faith in your abilities.'

She's glad someone does.

She asks him how he knows Cassy.

'Cassy ... refresh my memory.'

'The woman who first introduced me to you.'

'Ah yes, red hair. She auditioned with me once, but I didn't feel she had anything unique to offer the Circus. I don't employ actors. As you know, I'm seeking genuine, not contrived experience.'

Lucy notices a photo of a woman and a girl on a table in the corner. She goes over to look. They are smiling into the camera, their arms around each other, hair blown sideways across their faces. She glances over towards Phineas.

'Are these – ?'

'Yes.'

The girl has an elfin face and short dark hair. Lucy picks up the photo and looks more closely. There is a striking resemblance between her and this girl. She glances up at Phineas, but he has returned to his work. She turns around and goes back to her desk. He's starting to make more sense to her now.

Later, Phineas asks Lucy to tell him a story.

'My great-grandmother saw an angel when she was young.'

'What happened?'

'She was sick with tuberculosis, lying in her bed full of fever. One night an angel came to her and asked her if she was ready to leave, if she wanted to die.'

'And did she?'

'No. She told the angel she wanted to stay and so the angel left. When she woke up in the morning her fever had subsided and she was well again. It was a miracle.'

Then she asks him to tell her a story, and this is what he says:

'I was in St Andrew's here in Vancouver. It was an early morning in November, dark, like it always is here in the winter, a constant ceiling of cloud. You'll see …

'I was sitting in a pew in a dim alcove to the right of the altar. Rows of votive candles burned in front of me, casting a warm glow into the cold corner, filling the air with the smell of wax. The sound of rain was heavy on the roof, muffling the noises of the city outside. I closed my eyes and a feeling of well-being settled over me. I had the sensation of a thick blanket being placed across my back and shoulders.

'Then I felt myself lifting up and away from the pew, as if my body had become weightless. I opened my eyes and saw that I was floating towards the large stained-glass window behind the altar. It showed the Virgin Mary embracing an adult Christ. Both figures were positioned frontally, so that anyone looking at them would meet their gaze.

'I found myself hovering in front of this grand window through no will of my own. I was faced with these eyes, hers and his, and they held me there, transfixed, suspended in air. I don't know how long it lasted, but at some point I felt myself lowering, returning to the pew.

'I'm still not sure what happened and it hasn't happened since. I know there are many examples of levitating saints in Christian history – Joseph of Copertino, Teresa of Avila, others – but I'm not exactly what you would call a saint.

'Anyway, this is how the Holy Circus was born. I became interested in everything impossible. I began researching documented miracles of faith, strange occurrences that have happened to people over the ages with no scientific explanation.

'I put up ads for modern-day miracles, metaphysical anomalies, to come and share themselves with me and with the public. I grew to believe that my quest is to foster openness in these ironic times, when believing in the unexplained is considered unfashionable, and people's minds are closed by cynicism.

'And of course, there's always the possibility that I'm just crazy ... '

Lucy slides him a sideways glance. He's laughing, so she laughs, too.

After work, thoughts she can't keep down pop up like bubbles in water. The girl in the photo. Miracles. And especially Cassy. How she had hoped for something, someone to be there for her. A presence worth trusting. Instead she ended up with a fanciful creation, a fire-breathing chimera. Certainly not anything reliable.

And there's the ongoing anxiety of her changing body. Trying to grow, using her as a portal. Everything divided and dividing. The low but persistent background music to her life here that cannot be turned off. If only Levi –

Lucy catches herself and turns away. She walks to the kitchen, makes herself a cup of hot water and eats five grapes. She arranges her shells in straight lines on the window ledges. She takes two laxatives. She makes more lists.

༄

August 14, 1974

Wren,

Before your pregnancy, I would sit in the library, waiting for you to finish work. Borrowing tall stacks of books, anticipating long weekends spent together in bed reading. Losing ourselves in imaginary worlds.

I think of you reading to the twins when they were still in your belly. Resting the book on the top of the bulge, letting your voice float out over the shape of them. Even then, filling their heads with stories. Now, though they're not old enough to understand everything, I'm reading to them, too. I know it's what you would have done, raising our children on words.

I can hardly believe it's been over three years since I felt the warm air from your mouth against mine. I confess, I've taken to using your bath oil and soap. The smell of you on my skin. In this way, we still sleep together. I carry you to work in the mornings, under my clothes. I don't go anywhere without you next to me.

Lucy has gone down a size, just like Alice, shutting up like a telescope, curiouser and curiouser. She shops in the girls' department, buying new clothes, shirts with butterflies and flowers on them.

Sometimes she buys fashion magazines. Cuts out pictures of models in forests, their long hair lit by slants of sun coming through the trees, skirts the colour of bark, their bodies seeming to glow, unearthly. These photos are her company in the middle of the city – barely-there spirit-girls who flit through the trees, the rich greens of moss and ferns. She tapes the pictures to the inside of the medicine cabinet door in the bathroom. Her secret place. When she feels weak or faded, she opens the door to look and it strengthens something inside her.

She has decided not to think about Cassy. When she flits across her mind, Lucy puts her on a cloud and watches her float away. She doesn't want her in her head. She can control her appetites; she can turn Cassy off. She's just glad Cassy introduced her to Phineas. That's all.

To celebrate her new job and home, Lucy takes herself out to the opera. *Tosca*.

She wears a long lacy dress that she found in a thrift store on Cordova Street and dyed black. Topped off with a dark blue velvet cape and a rhinestone tiara nested in her hair, she makes her way through the wet streets. Swishing along beneath the trees in darkness, sweating a bit under her costume.

At the theatre, she sits back in her plush burgundy seat and breathes in the grand sense of space. *This could be my world*. Her hand moves to her throat and the lights dim.

The best moment is right before Tosca kills Scarpia with the knife he used to eat his dinner. Tosca languishes in Scarpia's salon, tortured with her task, her opulent necklace and hairpins glittering, singing, *'Art and love have always been my life … I have never hurt anyone.'* When Lucy hears that line, she bites her lip to keep from crying.

And then, on the way home, street comments: 'Oh, baby. So beautiful. You're looking so good, I could make love to you.' Followed by a long, slow whistle.

She knows that some singers don't speak during the day when they have an evening performance. When someone addresses them, they wave, saying nothing. They avoid cheese, meat, milk and cold drinks. They're allowed to abstain.

Lucy pretends to be a famous singer and walks quickly, ignoring the voices and the whistles. Holding her sparkling head high while she imagines a dinner knife flashing through the air to silence their ignorant leering.

Once past the voices, she returns to her own meandering thoughts. Beneath the pavement, under the city streets, the labyrinth of sewer pipes gushing onward. The world below the world. She can hear the surge of water, an invisible dark river coursing towards its destination of purification and rebirth. The ceaseless persistence of renewal.

She starts to walk faster, heading towards the ocean, opening her mouth to the salty breeze, taking off her tiara and feeling the air move through her hair. Blowing out all the cobwebs, the poison of being only looked at and not seen.

Back in the apartment, she lights candles and opens the balcony door wide. The air from the sea blows in and sculpts the wax into gothic shapes. She lets her voice uncurl slowly from her throat. Practicing arpeggios. Scales. Her voice rising, she climbs, becomes a nightbird, and soars over the buildings, away from the lights and the smell of cars. She flies alone in the dark over the ocean, over pods of whales, the clear tones ringing out across miles of shining black water reflecting the moon. She flies all night without tiring, returning to the city only when the sun begins to stain the horizon pink.

∝

January 19, 1975

Wren,

Finally, sitting down with you. Just finished cutting wood. The trail of wood chips across the floor from the woodshed. Crackle of the wood stove in the front room. The wind howling outside in the dark, sounding like it wants to come in.

There are only a few days a year when I curse my job and wish for the luxuries of a warm office, however dull. Today was one of them, my heavy nylon jacket feeling like it was made of tissue paper, the wet air crawling inside me, taking up residence in my bones. I couldn't get my wool hat to cover enough of my head, my feet were numb blocks inside my boots. My hands were the only warm part of me, shelled up to the forearm in my lined rubber gloves. Barely a reprieve for ten hours, just the continual crash of water over the side of the boat, the wind, the slicing through and through. Only two things will take this kind of chill out: a deep bath in water as hot as the day was cold, and the radiating warmth of two bodies entwined under sheets.

I remember when we wallpapered our room. Dense red roses from floor to ceiling on every side. You pulled me down with you, laughing into my beard. 'Let's be lovers in our own castle while the rest of the kingdom sleeps for a hundred years.'

Now it is you in the hundred-year sleep. Dreaming calmly, peacefully, until I can come to join you and we can wake up together.

∝

The nights have been long. Lucy sleeps and wakes, sleeps and wakes, fitful. The only way she can get back to sleep is if she lies on her side and presses her hands together under her head, as if she is praying. Her dreams are tattered multi-coloured rags tied to a fence. Levi. Her dad. Inescapable. She puts these dreams out of her mind as soon as she wakes, but they linger, pulling at her.

During the days she is nauseated, a strange greenish girl, black hair in a tangle. She doesn't have much of an appetite and can't seem to keep anything down. She takes consolation in the smooth dip of her abdomen, from one hip bone to the other. Like a hammock. The laxatives keeping everything under control.

She starts getting up earlier in the mornings, pushing down the nausea, going for long runs around the seawall. There are other joggers, a few people walking their dogs, but mostly she is alone with the ocean. Fresh air blowing into her head off the emerald body of the Pacific. Circling gulls. She feels all her edges, her feet against the path. She smells the trees.

It takes her about an hour to run the whole seawall. The first ten minutes are the worst, when she still feels thick and heavy, before her body finds a rhythm and the oxygen in her blood starts to take her higher. As if the salt water were a magnet pulling everything unnecessary out of her, until only the essential scaffolding remains. After these runs, she feels tired but victorious. Clean.

Sometimes, when she lets herself have a chocolate bar, she savours each bite, knowing it might be the only thing she'll eat that day. When she feels hungry, she drinks hot cups of water with lemon. This fills her stomach, warms her up, creates the feeling of a constant taking in. How can she be hungry if she's always taking in?

Yesterday, Phineas told her she was looking too skinny. He asked her if she was eating and she said of course and showed him the salad she brought for lunch. He said it didn't look like much and later she found a banana and an apple on the corner of her desk.

Today was a feast: half a head of iceberg lettuce, four pieces of raw cauliflower, two carrots. Half a can of tuna. Jasmine tea. She feels electric. She is walking on a very high thin fence with her arms out beside her. An airplane, perfectly balanced, aloft in the sky.

She daydreams about apricots sticky with syrup, green beans with bacon, mashed potatoes with butter and gravy, cake. Food from the old days.

Funny, though, lately her vision seems to be changing. Things off in the distance are looking blurry. She doesn't remember that from before. Maybe she needs glasses.

∞

July 11, 1976

Wren,

Moving my hands to my face, running my fingers over my cheekbones, around behind my ears. Along the base of my skull. I remember their skulls when they were babies, the lines of their fontanelles, the skin slightly sunken. How I held one of their heads in each hand and marvelled at the soft pulsing spots at the top of each one. So vulnerable, that place where they were poured into themselves. I closed my eyes and inhaled, as you would have – first one and then the other – breathing in the sweetish smell of them. Thinking, these babies are still wide open.

Remember the afternoon you conceived?

Our picnic dinner out on the feathery grass of the back field. June, the air hot and sticky. We were drinking wine, our mouths stained red with it, looking like we'd been sucking the blood from living things. You lay down against the nubbed cotton bedspread of your childhood, made by your mother's mother. Your nipples pushed up against the fabric of your light summer dress, my fingers moving over your collarbone. The warmth of your chest rising and falling, following the curve of your breast back across your ribs. The pale tufted hair of your armpits catching the sun as you raised your arms above your head. How we got drunk with each other, our hands, tongues, lips moving too slowly, never reaching far enough.

You sitting above me, the dress damp and crumpled beside us, your body shining with heat, your legs slipping over my hips. There was no one to be quiet for and we moved like hungry animals. How we both cried out when the twins slipped in between us.

How, later, you said, 'If I had died that moment, I couldn't have picked a better time.'

We were resting together, your head against my shoulder.

'You'll live to be ninety years old with me,' I told you, 'and we'll die at exactly the same moment.'

Everything was still shimmering with heat as the sun slowly lowered itself towards the treetops behind us. Gooseberry and red currant bushes lined the back fence, and the plum trees on the edge of the woods were heavy with fruit. The air smelled of goldenrod. All around, the grass was vibrating with the invisible movement of rabbits and snakes. We had caused the world to grow larger.

On her way to work, Lucy sometimes passes by the Asian rabbit man who lives near Phineas. He takes his pet rabbit on slow walks around the block, holding it in his arms close to his chest, like a baby. Both of them, so vulnerable somehow. Whenever she sees him, she blinks quickly and swallows hard to keep down the sudden tears that well up in the back of her throat.

She is at her desk in the office. Phineas paces in front of the window, concentrating on the carpet, brushing his dark hair out of his eyes with his hands. He mutters to himself, things she can't hear, sometimes nodding his head, sometimes stopping to stare out towards the mountains. This goes on for some time. The pacing is starting to drive Lucy crazy.

'Is there anything that you need help with?' she asks him.

He looks at her as if he is returning from a distant voyage.

'Help. Yes. Yes, but not yet. I have to write it down first.'

He goes to his desk and starts scribbling furiously onto a pad of paper with a pencil. The scratching sound the pencil makes is less distracting than his pacing.

'There,' he says. 'Can you type that up for me?'

She looks at the piece of paper he has handed her.

'I've decided I need to gather my thoughts together. Will you help me do that?'

His eyes are bright.

'Of course. I'll get started right now.'

He beams at her.

His handwriting is crabbed but she can make it out.

Topic: The Eventual Translucency of People

Hannah the x-ray woman may be a pioneer of the lighter days to come. Already, there are others like her, presaging the time when bodies will become so fine, so insubstantial, that they will be truly translucent …

The next day when Lucy arrives at work, Phineas says, 'Today is an outside day. I need you to come to the beach with me.'

So they go out walking, the mountains towering clear and cold across the water, the sun brilliant.

'What are we doing?' she asks.

'We're thinking. We're walking and thinking. Do you mind walking with me? Having you here helps me organize my thoughts.'

They continue on in silence for a while, Phineas looking mostly at the ground, Lucy watching crows dropping mussels onto the rocks from above to break open the shells.

'I've been thinking about maybe developing an act for the Circus myself,' he says, his voice quiet. She moves in closer to hear him. 'A kind of revisionist version of the minister I used to be, where I give short talks on subjects that interest me.'

She says she thinks it's a good idea and after a while they stop at a bench, where Phineas pulls out a pad and begins to write.

She pulls her coat closer around her. *What a strange job.* Everything about her life has this slightly unreal quality right now. Sometimes she isn't sure if she believes that any of it is really happening. *Maybe it's all a bizarre dream.* Her stomach contracts under her sweater. She closes her eyes and fills her lungs up with air. Pretends, an oxygen milkshake.

When Phineas tucks his paper away and stands to leave, Lucy is hugging herself with both arms and smiling. Relishing the feeling of lightness in her body.

'What's this one about?' she asks.

'I'm calling it *A Case Against Inbreeding*. It's a call to leave the geography of the charted and fertilize the world. To move beyond simple transgression into something truly innovative.'

His voice hangs in the air for a moment before being swallowed by the waves. When Phineas turns to look at her, Lucy is not smiling any more. Her face looks white and drawn.

She starts a Phineas list, a collection of phrases she hears him saying to himself, lines that stick in her mind.

Phineas #1:
> *invisible information moving finely*
> *antennae receiving*
> *messages across the curve of space*
> *Are you open? Is this coming through?*
> *bodies that become light*
> *lighter, lightest, until:*
> *disembodied*
> *you're all gone*
> *a spirit on air*

∽

August 27, 1976

Wren,

They were in the lake and on the dock all day today. Tonight, their faces glowed pink and tired in the firelight. There was the smell of burnt marshmallows, the pop of the fire, the heat against the chill of the night, the dew. The sound of the waves against the shore. An indigo sky full of stars. Cinders panting by the fire, a black shadow, her glinting eyes watching the trees. I told the children about a forest with a wizard who used to be a rabbit, elves and gnomes that lived in the carpet of ferns. All the talking animals and plants. Caves that open up from the ground like trap doors.

They leaned into each other listening, droopy-eyed. When I finally tucked them into bed, I smelled their hair. Pillows full of woodsmoke and sun all summer long.

೪

In the office, Phineas scratches away with his noisy pencil.

'What are you working on today?' Lucy asks him tentatively.

He looks up, his eyes glazed, the way they get when he writes his ideas.

'Simultaneous realities. Stories that go on side by side. Worlds that we inhabit concurrent with the world that we are in now.'

He smiles vaguely at her before bending his head down to continue.

Walking across the bridge on her way home, Lucy imagines that she is an acrobat.

Her body her religion. Tendon. Muscle. Strength. Concentration. She relies on the efficacy of wires and pulleys, the meticulousness of technicians, the firm grasp of her partner's hands, and the strength of her own body.

They descend together from the ceiling, suspended by cables, the sinew of his legs wrapped around her waist from behind. He clenches his thighs against her, pushing, and they spiral out, away from each other in mid-air. They turn and float, coming together, joining hands, swinging back, dancing on a string.

Other times they work in a group, as many as ten or twelve of them, dressed as sylphs in swamp-coloured body suits, shimmering with the iridescence of dried dog saliva. Their feet twirl up onto each other's shoulders, the one on the bottom widening her stance to support the increasing weight: a verdant tower, indivisible, the one mind, united into a single shivering reed.

People ask her, is it like flying? Yes, she says, as near as she's ever come. You could die, they say. Do you get scared? It's true, she responds. We're children of trust, believing that the cord will hold, that we'll make it through the next few minutes. We have to think this way.

∞

January 9, 1977

Wren,

Winter ice. Down with the rest of the crew in the smoke of the coffee room. The *Playboy* calendar above the table where we sometimes squeeze in a hand or two of cards between crossings.

'Do you ever think of me like that? As an object?' You asked me this once after I had given you a tour of the boat.

I didn't have to think before answering. 'No. No, of course not.'

Reaching over and kissing your neck. A simple gesture.

But now, now that your body is gone and you have no words to meet me with, I've been asking myself that question: are you an object to me? You're a woman I look at in photographs, trying to conjure up the exact timbre of your voice, the way you smelled. I imagine what it was like to hold you when you were here.

Is this wrong somehow? To still want you?

I have to confess, at times when the feeling is strong and has gone on for too long, I go outside, find a sheltered spot at the edge of the field, or in the trees, and give myself pleasure there with the wind and the sky all around me. I think of the times with you, your body and mine touched all over by air, by each other. The birds above us, your face against a backdrop of leaves or grass, your hair tangled, your cheeks full of blood. With these visions in my head, the longing moves out of my body for a brief moment, only to settle again in the space behind my ribs where it lives.

Forgive me.

It's impractical in all this rain, but Lucy buys an old fur coat at a vintage clothing store one day on her way home from work. She needs more protection from the damp air that has been creeping past her skin, climbing in beside her bones.

During these dark weeks, mist hangs thick in the trees shrouding the mountains, and there is often the familiar smell of woodsmoke. Her body responds automatically, her stomach in the clutches of longing, remembering home.

Winters out here are so different from winters back there. On the island, the silence of snow felt like it went on forever. Sometimes when she inhaled, her lungs would catch, and for an instant she could imagine never breathing again.

Carrying kindling in from the shed behind the kitchen, dropping chips along the way, tiny bits of wood to get caught in socks, nested in wool sweaters. The sound of feeding logs into the fire, the creak and clank of the stove door closing, the crackle of bark as it flamed. Standing with her hands out, letting her body absorb the heat. Cinders lying on the linoleum beside the stove until she got too hot and moved to a cool corner.

Now, on the balcony, looking out over the water, there is the unceasing rain, but everything is still green, alive and breathing. She can step outside in winter like this without shattering her lungs. Then, up from nowhere, a thought of Levi: *How is it for him, breathing the air where he is?* Her body crumples, remorse and sorrow falling out of her in a sudden stream of vomit she is powerless to contain.

One morning, they're in Phineas's car on their way to drop off some posters and brochures, when out of the blue he says, 'A basic Buddhist truth is you are what you see. What do you think of that?'

She shrugs. Keeps looking out the window. She feels cold. It hasn't stopped raining for seven days.

After work, Lucy passes a man whose lives on the street. Each day he is there on his stretch of sidewalk, under the open sky. He leafs through a tattered Sears catalogue, his hands grey with dirt. He scratches something onto a bit of paper with a ballpoint pen. He walks to the corner, his pants falling down, his buttocks a shocking band of white across the middle of his body. He keeps to himself, speaking quietly, occasionally tossing an arm up, gesturing to someone who isn't visible. Lucy doesn't know where he keeps his things. She doesn't know where he goes to the bathroom. Some days she sees a sleeping bag crumpled in a ball at the edge of the sidewalk, some paper cups, a sandwich, a few pennies.

As she passes by, she treads lightly. She is in someone else's home, after all. Phineas's words, boomeranging around her head like some kind of June bug trapped indoors on a spring night. *You are what you see.*

✎

March 23, 1977

Wren,

In the woods, winter is slowly giving way to the promise of spring. Your favourite time of year. Nights still cold and crisp, while the days are gradually warming up. Perfect for sugaring.

I pulled the twins on a toboggan attached to the back of the snowmobile. At the clearing, I cut up a fallen tree branch while they collected small pieces of wood and threw snowballs. When there was a tall pile of wood for the fire, we loaded up the toboggan and set out into the trees. Levi and Lucy helped me empty the long metal sap-collecting pails into the buckets. There was my voice and Lucy's as we sang, the sound of birds, the pervasive smell of sap, sweet and faint, mixed with the smell of slowly thawing earth. I hung the metal buckets back under the spouts for a few more days of gathering. Once we had visited all the trees, we took the sap back to the clearing and poured it into a big pot to cook.

I peeled oranges for us, sprays of juice arcing through the air. It's still true that an orange never tastes as good as it does out in the woods during winter. The fire crackled and the sap boiled. We sat on logs, eating our lunches from the flame-charred tinfoil wrappers. The sound of wind in the trees. Feet warming. Lucy humming between bites. Levi skimming the top of the sap whenever fire ash fell in.

There are the days when she wakes up to a flat leaden sky, the incessant sound of rain against the windows, the morning barely brighter than the night before. Her body with no will to move. She calls Phineas to tell him she's sick. Falls back asleep. Gets up in mid-afternoon and soaks in the bath, reading the books that she's bought, favourites from when she was a child, buckling the pages with her wet pruney fingers.

Minor earthquakes every day; that's what they say. Lucy feels the tremors like a needle sensitized to respond to the slightest movement. She feels the pressure, the blind thrust of the earth's elastic body, pushing out, pulling in, behaving unpredictably. She lies awake at night, staring into the darkness, thinking of the tectonic plates moving against one another, building up tension, until something has to give.

If she hadn't lost her witchy powers not so long ago, if they hadn't turned against her, she'd be thinking of some kind of spell to cast right now. A spell for a moment of stillness. A few words begging stability. She would whisper words of protection:

The earth will not be deformed.

The earth will endure without rupture.

The earth will not warp and collapse.

The earth will remain, all her rivers joined forever.

Instead, she makes promises to herself:

She will learn how to be a good witch again. She will think up new circus acts to do as charms against this twitching earth. She will stop eating entirely. She will drink only water, and if the earth threatens to engulf her, she will have already disappeared.

> *Symptoms of Seismic Activity:*
> *fifteen seconds of shaking*
> *pictures falling off walls*
> *teacups rattling in saucers*
> *people walking unsteadily*
> *small bells ringing*
> *difficulty standing*
> *waves on ponds*
> *books falling from shelves*
> *large bells ringing*
> *resulting aftershocks are felt for years*

The sun has set. Phineas and Lucy are walking again, down by the ocean's edge. Phineas skips stones across the surface of the water. Against the darkness of the Georgia Strait, huge tankers are lit up like floating chandeliers. Lucy imagines that they are hosting spectacular parties, full of sparkling people drinking champagne, making toasts to life. Dancing on the decks, brightly coloured flower petals and confetti all around.

'Do you feel the earthquakes?' she asks him. 'I feel tremors almost every night. I wake up because my bed is shaking. Do you feel them?'

Phineas leans down and picks up another flat stone.

'Yes, sometimes. But they don't bother me. Maybe you worry too much.'

She picks up a stone and throws it out in the water as far as she can. Her arm hurts. She picks up another stone and throws it further, arcing her body forward.

'Maybe I do.'

Topic: The Possibility of Immediate Apprehension
We have always wished for this: There is a book on the table. You reach out, touch the cover with your fingertips. Rest your palm for a moment on its surface. Your hand becomes a universe of eyes, your nerves, intelligent tunnels connecting to your brain. There is an immediate transfer of data, complete understanding and retention. You become a catalogue of philosophies.

∾

May 22, 1978

Wren,

Lately when the kids are doing their homework or have gone to bed and I finally get some time alone in my study, I've been rereading *Walden*. Remembering the reasons you and I decided to move to the country in the first place. Deciding to get out of the stink of the city and move to the island. Our own world, where we could live in the trees and fields. Where we could exist part of the time outdoors, part of the time in our imaginations, and, always, together.

I went to the woods because I wished to live deliberately, to front only the essential facts of life, and see if I could learn what it had to teach, and not, when I came to die, discover that I had not lived.

Reading it again makes my desire to write you even stronger. To record my own *Life in the Woods*.

To tell you about the increasing heat of the spring sun waking creatures from their snow-covered sleeps. How, everywhere, life is bursting out.

On the weekend we were outside. Me cleaning up some old brush, branches fallen down over the winter. The twins playing nearby.

I heard Lucy call out, and saw her pointing into the concrete foundation of the old barn beside the house. It was full of garter snakes. A carpet of them, knotted and writhing in the sun, warming their winter blood. Lucy exclaimed with delight, leaning in and picking one up, letting it twine around her arm and through her fingers. Levi frowned and climbed a tree, watching her from a distance.

They surprise me sometimes, our twins. So separate and so alike, simultaneously.

Lucy has an idea for a Circus act called Beauty in the Beast:

She enters the room in a giant bear costume. She starts to dance slowly, accompanied by discordant music played by some of the circus musicians, who are off to the side, hidden behind a curtain. As the music increases in speed and intensity so does her dancing, the bear head swaying in ever-widening circles, tongue lolling around loosely between the teeth in the big open mouth. When the music and dancing reach a frenzied pitch impossible to sustain, she flings herself to the floor and the musicians stop playing.

In the silence that ensues, she breathes deeply into her belly, slowing down her breath, using the force of her exhalations to propel her voice out of the veiled hole in the bear's head that masks her face. Her voice starts to spiral up like a snake from a basket, uncoiling slowly. It begins low and strong, like a monk's chant, as if from lungs used to climbing mountains. Gradually it builds, sound without words, until it fills the room and each person is frozen, flattened against the floor by the pure force of song.

And there is the act where she is a cosmonaut. Where she leaves the inner station for the outer station. Where she goes ballistic.

In this act, she boards her rocket, all smiles, in her sparkling metallic suit, ready to explore deep space, while the audience watches through video broadcast, observing her motion and flight behaviour.

She will be a space probe. Living life in the ether. Floating. Orbiting. Discovering uncharted worlds. Hoping to bring back good news, to manage a smooth landing. If and when she returns, she'll be careful to re enter the earth's atmosphere slowly, in order to avoid the bends.

Due to its grand scale, this performance would only be staged once.

F words:

>*fairy tale: a made-up story, usually designed to mislead*
>*fairy: a small, imaginary being with magical powers*
>*falter: stumble, stagger, go unsteadily*
>*familiar: a spirit held to serve or guard a person; a close friend or associate; sexually intimate*
>*fay: to fit or join closely, as two timbers, two twins*

Really, it isn't that bad, she tells herself. There are the occasional waves of nausea, but Lucy calms herself by practicing her breathing and writing more lists. She tapes them to the wall beside her bed and onto the living room walls. They are taking over the apartment.

She goes to the eye doctor and it turns out her eyes are weaker. She orders contact lenses. When she asks the doctor why this is happening now, he tells her he isn't sure, but not to be concerned because her eyes are healthy. He says sometimes it happens as people get older or when they're under unusual stress. She doesn't tell him about her freakbelly.

Topic: Karma of Parasites

> *We are the congregation of birds on the back of the rhinoceros, feasting on her delicious supply of bugs. Revelling in our glorious plastics, our vaporous, ephemeral technologies. Forgetting our elemental selves. Blind to the cycles of our ancestors. Their bodies condensing as clouds, falling as rain into our palms, onto our tongues. The great return.*

∽

March 7, 1979

Wren,

Cinders has been missing for two days now. The last thing any of us saw was the black shape of her, standing near the road at twilight. You know how she was always a car chaser.

I remember when we went to the pound and picked her out, years ago. How tiny she was, the runt of the litter. How we both fell in love with her right away. When you said she was as black as cinders, she was named, just like that.

I told the twins that she had probably run away to join the wolves. We still hear them howling at night, and sometimes we see one skulking around the edges of the forest or silhouetted in the back field.

I think they believed me, though Levi asked a lot of questions about what would happen if she died somewhere. Would her body start to smell? Would she rot? Would she be eaten by other animals? He has quite an imagination – afraid of snakes but not death.

They both kept moping around the house so much that I told them we could get a cat as a replacement. That seemed to cheer them up. We piled in the truck and went to the McGregors' where there was a new litter. They each picked one. Both black, a male and female.

With you here, we'd be a perfectly balanced family.

Lucy and the stigmata man, Dominic, are outside after rehearsal, on the stairs of the fire escape. The openings in Dominic's hands have stopped bleeding and have begun to scab over. Lucy breathes in the night air while he smokes. The sky is a black piece of felt, punctured with pinpricks of light.

'Are you Catholic?' she asks him.

He glances at her quickly before answering, flicking the ash of his cigarette over the metal railing. 'Agnostic,' he answers.

'So, why you then?'

He blows smoke rings towards the moon. He doesn't look anything like the bearded white man with the sad blue eyes Lucy recalls seeing in bible story pictures. He has dark skin and eyes, and short, bleached blonde hair. He wears a silver hoop in his nose.

'You mean, why aren't I a saint or a priest, or a visionary? Why would a miracle of faith visit an unbeliever?'

She tries her question again. 'I mean, what do you make of it? Has it changed your life?'

He stubs out the butt of the cigarette under the heel of his boot and lights another.

'Well, it's given me a job. And a hiding place. No one bothers you when you're an artist. Now, if I was Joe Godfearing Everyman with his stigmata, the media and church would be all over me. As a performer, I'm left alone. No one believes it's real. It's just an act, right? Besides, everyone's getting stigmata these days. Being chosen by God isn't the oddity it used to be.'

'Do they hurt?'

'They tingle, that's it. And they're a nuisance. I have to wear gloves. People tend to stare.'

Lucy looks down at her own smooth, white hands.

'I want to be in the circus, but I don't have an act,' she tells him.

Dominic inhales, holding the smoke in his lungs for a few seconds before exhaling.

'Maybe you should give birth onstage. No one's done that yet. Goodnight.'

Lucy looks up, but he's already making his way down the fire escape. She watches his back, listening to the crunch of his shoes on the gravel as he walks down the alleyway and disappears into the dark.

Fantastic Creatures:
> *Centaur: a monster having the head, arms and torso of a man united with the body and legs of a horse*
> *Harpy: a winged monster with the head of a woman and the tail, legs and talons of a bird, that fouls or seizes its victim's food and carries off the souls of the dead*
> *Alien: a member of a foreign nation, tribe, people, etc.; one estranged or excluded*
> *Baby: a very young child of either sex; an infant; one who looks or acts like a child; small; diminutive; miniature; a young woman, a sweetheart*

November 16, 1979

Wren,

Our son the artist. The other day he found an abandoned bird's nest with tinsel woven through it. He was sitting at the table during dinner drawing it in his notebook. I had to remind him to eat. Later, I noticed the nest arranged with his collection of rocks on the shelf beside his bed.

He's always pulling a pencil and paper from somewhere in the folds of his clothes, quietly sketching. First he copied pictures from books, teaching himself about the thinness and thickness of lines, the subtleties of tone and value. Following the path of the more experienced hand. Now I often see him out in the fields, drawing birds, insects, trees, the world around him. I think maybe it's time for lessons. Both of them. Lucy is always making up songs …

I can imagine it: we'll go into town, Levi at art, Lucy at singing. I'll sit, drinking coffee and reading in some patch of sun, while our children grow more brilliant.

Lucy is full of holes. Space needing to be filled with something. Someone. Now a baby grows there. Trying to fill her up. And sometimes, despite all her pushing down and away, she catches herself talking to it in her head. As if it can hear her. *Maybe you will be born with two heads. Homunculus. Ha ha. Maybe you hold all the answers. Quick, baby, send a telegram out through my umbilicus. I must have word*

She wakes up with a start at three am. *Is someone here?* She feels a presence, something moving, a shadow. Leaning over, she turns on the light beside the bed and looks around the room. The curtains shift slowly with the breeze through the open crack of the glass doors, and there is the streaming sound of rain. Nothing more.

She walks into the kitchen and puts on the kettle, checking the closets and under the bed while she waits for the water to boil. She lights a white candle, then turns out the lamp and climbs back into bed. The room flickers as she sits, cross-legged, propped up against her pillows, the steaming cup in her lap. She finds herself thinking of her young mother. What it must have been like, if she knew it was happening, if she'd had a chance to hold either one of them before she died.

Long after the mug is empty and the candle has burned down, she remains awake, staring out at the sky. Dawn creeps in and the rain stops. The clouds are parting when she sinks back under the sheets and closes her eyes.

Fantastic Creatures, continued:
> *Siren: partly human, female creature that lures mariners*
> > *to destruction by her irresistible singing*
> *Sylph: an elemental spirit of the air; a slender graceful woman*
> > *or girl*
> *Sibyl: a woman who lives in or on caves and utters advice*
> > *and prophecy in ambiguous wording under the*
> > *often frenzied inspiration of the gods*
> *sibylsibylsibyl sibilant sibyline sibling*

January 14, 1980

Wren,

You'd be proud. We've been working our way through *Myths and Legends of the World*. Prometheus stealing fire from heaven, Pandora loosing evil on the world, the love potion of Tristan and Iseult, the Gorgon's head …

Tonight Levi asked me what the difference is between a myth and a legend.

'They're both stories,' I said. 'But legends are based on events that really happened, while myths are usually made-up.'

His brow wrinkled and he pursed his lips like he does when he is trying to understand something.

'But how do you know which is which?' he asked. 'Can't some myths be legends and some legends be myths?'

'There are people, historians and cultural anthropologists, whose job it is to figure out these things,' I told him. 'They look at the stories and the history of a place or people, and they match things up.'

'But I don't see how they know for sure what's real and what's pretend,' he persisted.

I nodded. 'Sometimes it's hard to know the difference.'

Then Lucy piped up, saying that she liked the one about the box, and Levi corrected her: 'Pandora's box.'

'Yeah,' Lucy said. 'Pandora. She put the lid back on but it was too late, and all the badness was let out, and only hope was left. So the people always had hope, even though the world was full of problems, all because she opened this one box.'

∞

Phineas comes into the office, nods his head distractedly in Lucy's direction, takes his jacket off a hook on the wall, and heads back outside. She can hear him talking to himself.

'You get tired. You need a rest. You have to lie down in a quiet room where no one can find you … '

Night again. So soon after the meagre light of all these cloudy days.

Lucy wanders up and down the aisles of the small grocery store, scanning the shelves, looking for the food that will fill her. Eating with her eyes. Between the juice and the butter, there is a display piled high with clear plastic containers. Her fingers skim the tops of the round lids; nuts, chocolate macaroons, gumdrops, yogourt-covered raisins, seeds, candied fruit. Her hand hovers, passes by, then returns to a container of thin white wafers. Ingredients: Water, flour, salt. She chooses the ones that are least broken and takes them to the cash.

On the way home she stops at the liquor store and buys a bottle of red wine. Something from Bulgaria called St Stephen's Crown. She likes the way the bottle looks, old and dark, evoking monasteries, burning lanterns, the sound of heavy robes rustling down corridors.

At the apartment, she spreads a scarf flat on the floor and lights a candle. Taking one of the cups she bought in Chinatown, she fills it with wine and sets it down on the scarf. Kneeling, she closes her eyes and places one of the wafers on her tongue. She shuts her mouth and pushes the wafer up against her palate where it softens and begins to disintegrate. Then she brings the wine to her lips, letting it fill the cavity of her mouth and slowly leak down the back of her throat, warm and languid.

Before she falls asleep, she remembers a time when she was younger.

She was lying on her back in the tree house, looking up into the green ceiling of leaves, balancing a small glass container with an ornate silver lid on her chest. It used to hold rose-scented cream, and it still smelled like the perfume. Inside, there was cotton batting and a sparkling brooch that belonged to her mother, and to her grandmother before that. She lifted the brooch up to the light and sent dozens of reflections bouncing onto the tree trunk and into her face.

She could spend hours lying on her back against this floor, surrounded by the whispering coolness of leaves, the calm warmth of wood. Her own, sparkling world. If only she could get back there somehow. To the time before the dreams where Levi's face is suspended above hers, too close. And now, so far.

Disappearances:
the skinny
pencil-thin
splinter-girl
shaving off
wastrel
whisper
secret
shhhh

✂

April 3, 1980

Wren,

We almost lost Levi.

Even now, a full day later, fear cuts into me as I think about it.

He was going blue by the time they came with the oxygen. Lucy was quiet and tense beside him, holding his hand, her own turning white. I coached him: 'In and out, nice and slow, your lungs are expanding, filling with air, you're calm and relaxed. Don't worry, they'll be here soon. Calm and relaxed.' Trying not to listen to his rasping asthmatic lungs, seeing his eyes widen as his breathing grew more shallow.

But they did come, gave him oxygen and kept him breathing during the ferry crossing, until the hospital, where they gave him medication, and he was fine. He is fine.

I didn't start shaking until after, when we were on our way home, gripping the steering wheel harder to steady myself. Checking on him every few seconds through the rearview mirror, as he curled into Lucy on the back seat. 'He's all right, Dad,' she said. 'He's resting.' Her hand across his shoulders.

I was still shaking when I went to bed. It didn't stop until I fell asleep, even then, fitfully recurring as I tossed and turned my way towards dawn. Too close. It was much too close. I don't know what I'd do if I lost another one of you.

She asks Rosa the bird woman out for lunch because she wants answers.

'How do you get them to come and land on you? What do you do?' Lucy asks her.

She expects Rosa to eat like a bird, too, but instead she orders steak. When she presses her fork and knife into the meat, watery blood oozes out onto the plate.

'Does a magician explain her rabbit?' Rosa pulls a strand of long blonde hair from her mouth, replacing it with a forkful of steak. Her lips glisten with juice as she chews, keeping her eyes on Lucy.

She can feel herself blushing.

'A single rabbit and a room full of butterflies and birds seem like two different things to me,' Lucy says quietly, trying to avoid a tone of confrontation.

'They do, don't they?' Rosa moves a melting pat of butter over a mound of mashed potatoes. 'Except that rabbits have big floppy ears for hearing and birds don't. How do you think birds hear?'

She is playing Lucy for a fool. Avoiding the question. Lucy takes another sip of her water and rearranges the salad greens on her plate before answering.

'I think that birds have tiny antennae on the sides of their heads, invisible to the human eye. I think that birds are telepathic. I think that birds have a sophisticated group mind, and I think that you know something about how that mind works.'

Rosa smiles. The delicate bones of her face are dwarfed by her loose blonde hair and the expanse of her mouth. Lucy can sense the reality of her skeleton, the formula of her body nothing but a loose conglomeration of skin, tissue and viscera without the strength of bones to give her a shape.

'You miss him terribly, don't you?'

Lucy's elbow slips off the edge of the table where she is resting it, and she quickly repositions herself.

'You know who I'm talking about,' Rosa continues before Lucy has a chance to respond. 'And your father and mother. You miss all of them, constantly. That's why you're not eating.' She motions towards Lucy's salad with her steak knife.

Lucy starts to gather up her jacket and bag quickly, without looking at Rosa, though she can feel her eyes, sharp and intense, burning past her hair into her scalp.

Rosa continues to address Lucy as she walks towards the door. Lucy cannot hear what she is saying. She imagines that Rosa is a TV, a talking head on mute. She doesn't have to listen. She just has to walk away.

⁂

July 15, 1980

Wren,

I've been spending time with your kind. Denizens of the air:

Black-Capped Chickadee: *Parus atricapillus*. Small, tame acrobats. *Dee-dee-dee*.

Purple Martin: *Progne subis subis*. Blue-black. Sparrow-sized. Long, slim wings and graceful flight. Voice: throaty and rich. *Tchew-wew*.

Flicker: *Colaptes auratus*. Deeply undulating flight. Black 'whiskers.' A loud *klee-yer*.

Yesterday I asked Lucy to empty the compost bucket. An hour later she came to me in the woodshed where I was chopping some kindling for the stove, holding a piece of paper in her hands.

'A poem by Lucy Morgan,' she said, her face straight and serious. She cleared her throat and began to read. She recited a long rhyming list, about all the sorts of treasures a young girl can find in a compost heap. I remember some of them: mouldy old bread, a worm without a head; potato peels and bugs, slippery slimy slugs; some rusty old nails, a family of five snails.

When I told her that I thought it was wonderful, she beamed. She asked if I thought she should write more poems, and I said yes, absolutely. And so she ran inside with her pencil and paper, calling out to Levi that she had something to read to him.

Strange to admit, but sometimes I envy them. The bond they have. The way they share almost everything. Like you and I used to.

∽

Lucy's body is full of fault lines, invisible subduction zones. The plate of her past sinking dangerously beneath the plate of her present. A ridge of volcanoes set to erupt along her spine. Unchecked, she will rise up out of the sea and form new islands. She will leak channels of fire.

She only eats the most simple foods now. Fruit, steamed vegetables, water, the odd bowl of rice: these are the substances that deliver her to the ecstatic place she loves. The lightest food, and the joy of running beside the ocean, feeling her body move with the wind – this is what is building her into her most essential form. Running gives her the oxygen her cells crave as it streams into her body on the air. With each inhalation and exhalation she repeats it: *I am pure, I am pure, I am pure.*

At work, Lucy is typing up another piece of paper that Phineas has given her. She has started to wear baggier clothes to avoid further comments about her body. To give her more privacy. She gets up to go to the kitchen and has to hold the edge of the desk to steady herself. She feels weak in the legs. Lightheaded.

Phineas looks up from his work. 'Are you all right, Lucy?'

She sits down again. The solidity of the chair beneath her legs and buttocks, holding her up.

'I'm not used to these new contact lenses yet. I think they're affecting my sense of balance. I'll be fine in a couple of minutes.'

'Maybe you should pray to your namesake, the patron saint of eyesight.'

'Who's that?' Lucy says, closing her eyes and resting her fingertips lightly on her eyelids.

'Saint Lucy. She was quite something: she healed her mother who was dying of a hemorrhage. She was sentenced to death by fire, but wouldn't burn. And before she was beheaded by her suitor, she plucked out her eyeballs as a gift for him and they were immediately replaced by a new pair of eyes. In Latin, her name means *light.*'

Lucy stands up again and takes her coat from the back of her chair.

'It's lunchtime. I'm going out for a walk.'

On the path beside the water, she strides quickly, swinging her arms.

Up ahead, coming towards her is a woman with red hair. Lucy holds her breath. *Cassy?* She is the right height, has the same jerky body movements. Lucy looks for an alternate pathway, an escape route. There isn't one. As the woman approaches, Lucy's heart beats faster and her palms begin to sweat. Then she sees her. It isn't Cassy after all. A different red-haired woman entirely.

The woman passes without looking at her and Lucy sighs with relief. Her heart is in her throat. She is shaking. She sits on a bench to collect herself, taking deep breaths. Holding back tears.

She gives up on paper and starts writing directly on the walls of the apartment.

Standing back, she looks at her words. *Maybe these lists are all really songs. Maybe I need to sing them. Tristia: Songs of Sadness.*

Topic: Techniques for Achieving Ecstatic States
   1. Make an ink drawing on your left hand.
   2. Write your petitions before the setting sun.
   3. Understand animism as a foundational tenet in all
       circumstances requiring balance.
   4. Consider the future existence of humans with blue skin.
   5. Repeat the formula seven times.
   6. Send the truthful seer out.

∽

May 3, 1981

Wren,

Rise free from care before the dawn, and seek adventures … Grow wild according to thy nature … So says Thoreau.

I was digging around out in the back garden today, getting it ready for spring planting, and I found what looks like an old jawbone of a dog. The teeth are loose and rattling in their bone casing. It's hard to tell how old it is. Too old to be Cinders's. Who knows how many animals have lived and died here. The earth is held together by burials.

Red-Winged Blackbird: *Agelaius phoeniceus*. Red epaulets at the wing-bends. Gurgling *konk-la-ree* or *o-ka-lee*. Last note high and quavering.

⁂

Lucy lies on the floor of the apartment listening to the songs of humpback whales on her Walkman. How surprising that whales still exist. Something so huge, with secrets and systems that elude humans no matter how many studies are done. Imitating their voices with her own, she opens her mouth and sings. Squeaking arcs. Grunts and pips. Echoing cries. Saltwater flush. A primordial sadness.

She decides to go to them, to lay her head on the sand that is the floor of their home, and listen.

Packing a few things into her knapsack, she heads towards the beach. She watches the sunset with her back against a log, eats the apple and carrot she brought with her, and then finds a sheltered spot on the sand behind some rocks, hidden by overhanging blackberry bushes. She climbs into an old sleeping bag she found in the apartment and uses her rolled-up sweater as a pillow.

Resting there, imagining that she can hear their songs through the waves, she feels herself being pulled down into sleep. Surrounded by the sweet, earthy smell of blackberry bushes and cedar trees. Invisible and safe.

In the morning she wakes early and crouches behind some bushes to pee. The sky is beginning to lighten and the beach is empty when she strips to her underwear and runs into the water, inhaling sharply at the cold, then diving in and swimming a few strokes. She swims, front crawl, backstroke, sidestroke, until her limbs start to go numb.

She scans the beach and the path higher up. Still no one. Running back to the shore, she pulls off her underwear and quickly wraps herself in the sleeping bag, shivering, the flannel velvety against her skin. She curls up in a ball behind the rocks and watches the sky grow brighter, until she stops shaking. Glancing around one last time, she pulls on her clothes and packs up. She wants warmth, hot coffee, the calm certainty of a thick paper cup held steaming between her hands.

Her hair is still wet when she enters the café on Denman Street. She gets a non-fat latté and settles into a chair by the window, slipping off her sandals and tucking her socked feet up under her skirt, the cup nestled close to her chest.

All of these people probably slept in a bed last night. Four walls around. Door locked. Once you sleep out under the sky with nothing protecting you, what is there to be scared of?

A woman with white hair and scarlet lipstick sits at a nearby table having cake and coffee. She's dabbing at her nose with an embroidered handkerchief, pushing her glasses up closer to her eyes.

Lucy smiles at her and she smiles back, motioning with her hand to the chair across from her.

'What would you like, dear? Some cake, a danish?' She pulls her wallet out, jingling coins and the many charms on her gold bracelet.

'I'm okay.' Lucy holds up her coffee cup.

The woman scoffs, waving her hand. 'All you girls are too thin. A woman's got to have some curves!'

She gets up and buys Lucy a piece of carrot cake. 'Here, this has vegetables in it. Eat up, sweetheart.'

A woman of independent means. Clear blue eyes. Her face old, wrinkled, beautiful.

She opens her purse and shows Lucy a black and white photograph of a young girl standing in a field of grass, smiling at the camera.

'This was me. Taken in France when I was a girl. Croissants and cream sauces. Big bowls of milk and coffee. People in this country don't know how to live … '

She rustles a bottle of perfume out of her bag, sprays herself once on each wrist, then gathers herself up, rings and bracelet clattering. She pinches Lucy's cheek quite hard, leans close and looks her in the eyes.

'Prepare yourself, darling. Earthquakes can happen at any time. And remember, the last thing the world needs is more invisible women,' she says in a gravelly voice.

Types of Women:
> *virgin: an undefiled woman, spotless*
> *virago: a noisy, sharp-tongued woman; woman of extraordinary*
>   *strength and courage*
> *wanton: an unruly woman, hard to control*
> *fury: an angry or malignant woman*
> *hag: an ugly woman; a witch*
> *gorgon: a frightening or repulsive woman*
> *absent: a woman who is not there; one who has left*

Memories. Rising up despite all her best efforts at suppression.

Lucy was fifteen. She was in the woods beside the house, where the ground dipped down, near the rock caves. She lay in a pile of leaves with David Parker, his hand making its way from her waist up the front of her sweater. Before he reached her breast she put her hand over his.

'No. Just kissing. That's it.'

Her voice was firm, piercing the stillness of the trees. He wasn't going to argue with her.

'Okay. Sorry.'

His hand stayed there over her belly, while their tongues probed and flickered. Chickadees and blue jays called in the branches over their heads. On the edge of the woods, out of the corner of her eye, she thought she saw a shadow moving, melting into the trees.

Later, they had finished dinner and their father had gone off to his study like he usually did. After being quiet and strange all evening, Levi finally spoke.

'I saw you in the caves today.'

Lucy looked at him, holding his eyes in her gaze. She didn't say anything.

'I saw you there with David Parker.'

His face was turning red.

'It's nothing to get upset about.'

He looked at the floor, beetle-browed, and pulled at a loose thread on the knee of his jeans. Said nothing. Kept moving his finger in small circles over the nub of thread, not looking at her.

'What do you expect? Am I supposed to be a nun or something? I'm your sister, remember?'

Her voice was too loud. She was crying. She wiped the tears away hastily, closed her eyes and took a deep breath.

'All we did was kiss anyway. It's not like I'm going to marry him.'

Levi was silent. He looked at the floor, nodded and left the room.

∞

July 17, 1982

Wren,

A hot, humid day that started early with sun, and grew black with clouds by afternoon. We all wore the lightest dress-up clothes we could, Levi in green overall shorts with a white shirt, Lucy in a pale blue dress with elephants on it. She had pulled her hair into two shiny braids, tying one with a yellow ribbon, and one with a light blue ribbon the same colour as her dress. My thin cotton pants and shirt hung heavy and damp against my skin as we got in the truck to drive to the recital.

It was at the United church in town, under that lush canopy of trees, their branches tossed and swirled by the wind as it picked up momentum under a darkening sky. The sound of the leaves moving against each other was like thousands of pieces of paper talking, a conversation in green.

We entered the old building and found seats near the back, the whole place smelling of aged wooden pews, yellowing hymnal pages. I felt instantly sleepy, forced myself to sit with my back flat against the back of the pew, at attention while the children performed. The heat from my body pushed up the smell of your soap from my skin, so that I felt you there. Sitting beside me on the hard wood, your hand in mine.

The faces of the children were glowing, shimmering with a fine sheen of sweat while they played and sang. Lucy was marvellous, despite the thunder and wind that tried to drown her voice.

But somehow it rose above the storm, fine and slender, like a tightrope for us all to balance on.

༥

Lucy goes to bed early, before the sun sets, exhausted, too tired to answer the ringing phone, a heaviness in her stomach. When she wakes in the night with cramps like she's never experienced before, she switches on the light and reaches down to find her legs sticky with blood. Lying there, feeling her body contract with each wave of pain, she knows that the baby is flying off. Each wave of cramping seems worse than the one before. She is curled in a ball, rocking herself back and forth. She waits for a lull in her abdomen and gently lifts herself out of bed and to the bathroom. She pulls off her underwear and swallows two painkillers.

On the toilet, after a particularly strong cramp, she reaches down between her legs to find a mass. Scarcely formed, but still recognizable, is a *thing*. A fetus. She holds it there, dripping on the toilet seat, frozen. She can't just flush it away. She stares at it, her mind racing, until she knows what to do.

Hunched over, running warm water in the sink, she slides the tiny body in and washes it, lays it on a clean towel. It looks naked and exposed. More like a fish than a person. Dark spots where the eyes would have been. As if it's asleep.

She stays in the bathroom, huddled over the toilet, as more blood leaves her body. She opens her legs to look. Stringy. Membranes. *Where did my body get this much blood?* Fascination and repulsion punctuate the pain. And then, fear. *Is this what it was like for my mother? Am I going to die?*

Finally, when the cramps have slowed, she showers and puts on a fresh pair of pyjamas, folding a clean dishtowel into her underwear to soak up the blood.

In the living room, she takes incense sticks out of a sand-filled bowl on the floor. Scooping with both hands, she spreads a layer of sand in the bottom of a small cedar box and lays the cool body of the fetus inside it. Slowly, her eyes glazed and drooping, she fills the box with more sand until there is no trace left of the body. Putting dead things in boxes, just like when she was a child. Saving them for later. A beetle. A butterfly. A tiny, curled-up person. Peaceful and still. She ties the box closed with a cotton scarf, slides it up against the wall, and sits, her eyes shut, without moving.

Finally, numb from the painkillers, she leaves her vigil near the box and stands up, managing to change the sheets before collapsing into bed, exhausted.

She has just fallen asleep when there is a knock at the door. Phineas. Lucy stands, hunched over, looking at him. She's wrapped in a blanket, the loose corkscrew of her hair framing her face.

He cocks his head, taking her in, his eyes gentle. 'You didn't answer the phone. I wondered if something might be wrong.'

When he strokes her face lightly with his hand, Lucy fights back the urge to cry, her chest a torrent of moths. She turns around and crawls back under the blankets while Phineas boils the kettle.

He brings out two steaming cups and hands one to her. She sits up a bit, cradles the cup against her belly, comforting herself with the heat.

'I have something for you,' he says, pulling a small black bag from his pocket. He presses it into her hand. She opens it to find a silver chain with a medallion of a saint on it. She holds it up.

'Who is it?' she asks.

'Saint Jude, patron saint of lost causes. It belonged to my mother. Her mother gave it to her when my father died during the war. To bring back what had been lost. I thought it might do you more good than me.'

There is also a piece of paper. It is thin and tattered with age and repeated foldings:

A Prayer to Saint Jude

I honour and invoke you as the patron of hopeless cases, of things despaired of.

Pray for me who am so miserable; make use, I implore you, of this particular privilege accorded to you, to bring visible and speedy help, where help is almost despaired of.

Come to my assistance in this great need, that I may receive the consolations and succor of Heaven in all my necessities, tribulations and sufferings.

Lucy fastens the chain around her neck. The medallion rests in the flat hollow between her breasts. She touches it, her fingers tracing the outline of Jude's body, the drape of his robe. She likes the way it feels.

Closing her eyes, Lucy lets herself sink back into the pillows. She drifts in and out of sleep. She can hear Phineas talking quietly as if he's far away, at the end of a long padded tunnel. His musical voice wrapping around her head like a crown.

'Here is a story:

'Back in the days before gravity had fully taken hold on this planet, there lived a flock of birds the colour of alabaster. Over time they were losing too many of their group to the perils of flying in the earth's atmosphere without the full force of gravity to prevent them from floating off and disappearing into outer space. To save themselves, they quickly evolved the species-preserving ability to spin a spider-like silk out of their hindquarters, which they attached to a solid earthbound object before beginning any flight. This thread was exceedingly fine and strong, billowing out behind the alabasters like kite strings in the wind.

'Over time and many successful flights, the air became so tightly woven with the shimmering silver threads that the gravity problem was resolved, and the earth's atmosphere became a safe place for all winged creatures to fly in without fear of slipping into the void. The alabasters were then able to stop spinning their threads.

'Yet, despite the fact that they ensured not only their own survival but that of all birds, these spinners are rarely seen. In fact, their existence today is the subject of great dispute. Some say that they never existed at all.'

There is a silence. Phineas leans in close and speaks softly beside her ear.

'I know that you have left many things behind in an effort to remake yourself. Perhaps you wished to die giving birth to the child. To rise up and rid yourself of a body entirely. But even flying things must have roots, invisible threads that keep them in the earth's atmosphere. Sometimes it seems like the hardest part of living is admitting the necessity of roots. But once you do, you may be surprised by the smoothness of your flight.'

II

The Sweet Smell of Embalmment

LEVI'S APARTMENT IS IN THE MCGILL GHETTO, close to the Royal Victoria Hospital. Outside the bedroom window is a building with a thick red brick smokestack that reaches into the sky. The building throbs and whirs, a monster belly taking in and spewing out, constantly cycling. Heavy grey smoke billows from the smokestack at night, a visible column under the stars and moon. What do hospitals do with body parts from surgeries and accidents? He imagines autoclaves, hyper-incinerators, concrete tumbling furnaces, airtight drums, ashes. He wonders if there is anything left over.

Trucks come and go at all hours, their reverse signals beeping, diesel fumes blowing in his open window. A sound like a table saw. A manhole cover being lifted and replaced, lifted and replaced.

When he first moved in, the constant puffing and grinding sounds kept him awake at night, but it didn't take long to get used to them. Now they are almost a comfort. He has learned to sleep more deeply.

Levi finds himself here in Montreal with the small body of a papier mâché frog appearing in his hands. As his fingers move, shaping, smoothing, he thinks of the sensitivity of frogs, how they breathe through their skin. He is making snakes, too. Snakes, after so many years of hating them. And there are birds, soft and fragile, made of layered cheesecloth. He makes them small and crouched, their wings held tight against their bodies. Poised for flight, or life, or death.

He builds all these bodies from scratch, working on them day and night, sleeping as little as possible. Lining them up under the windows when they're finished. A menagerie. A strange family made of newsprint, cloth and glue. He will build them a shelf with discrete compartments where each animal can have its own space. A sort of postmodern nest. He will put a piece of glass across the shelves to shield them. So they are still visible but won't fall out or get lost.

There is a young blind woman who lives in the apartment next to his. Levi has seen her coming and going with her seeing-eye dog. Her light brown hair falls loose around her head and shoulders. Levi hears her singing through the ventilation shaft that runs through the centre of the building. She sings when she goes up and down the stairs with a clear and innocent voice that gives him a pain somewhere deep inside his body.

⁂

21 Sept. 1989

Dear Dad,

Things are going well. I've settled into school and am quite busy. This city is alive with the passion of many cultures – it inspires me. I made the right decision to come.

How are you? Any word from Lucy? I expect not. I'm sure she's fine, though. She's smart and knows what she's doing. I'm sure of it.

I live on Rue Ste Famille. Saint Family. Lucy would probably say that's good luck or something.

Must get back to work. I'll write again soon.

Love, Levi

⁂

December 5, 1982

Wren,

I don't know how to do any of this. So clumsy. Maybe it's because I've noticed Lucy's breasts beginning to grow. Maybe the twins just seem older somehow. Whatever the reason, I thought I should initiate 'the talk' with Levi.

I went into his room this evening when he was doing his homework and sat on the edge of his bed. He looked up at me, expectant and patient at the same time. Looking much more calm than I felt.

'Levi, I thought we should have a little chat about, um, sex,' I started, clearing my throat of several frogs.

His face turned red and he looked down at his lap.

'What about it?' he said.

'Well, I wanted to make sure you understand it, how it's done. I mean, what it's all about.'

I couldn't believe how inane I sounded. I wiped my sweaty palms on my pant legs. He didn't say anything, so I continued.

'Do you understand what happens to a man's body when he is, um, aroused? That his penis –'

'Dad,' he stopped me. His face was still red. 'They teach us that at school, you know. In sex ed class. I know about babies and all that.'

I felt relief flooding through me. Someone else had done the job.

'Do you think your sister knows?' I asked him.

'Sure she knows. They teach the girls separately from the boys, but she knows.'

'Well, good. That's fine.' I stood up. 'Now, of course, if you have any questions, if there's anything at all you don't understand, you know that you can come to me, right?'

'Yes, Dad. I know.'

I ruffled his hair before leaving the room. It had been so much easier than I had anticipated.

∞

Levi's instructors have been recommending books, religious and mythological books like the stories his father would read to Lucy and him before bed. Strange what sticks in your memory. Details that are hard to put into words. The feeling of a frog in the hand.

The lofts in the barn were always dusty, hay scattered over the intermittent floorboards. They didn't go up there much – you never knew if you were going to stick your foot through a hole. The walls were hung with old rusted tools. The empty stalls below echoed with the ghosts of dead animals, their disembodied voices reverberating through the still air of quiet afternoons.

In the field beyond the barn, a log doubled as an airplane, and the grass vibrated with hundreds of small orange butterflies. In spring, the ditch was a river of treasures that they waded through in rubber boots. They cupped the sun-warmed water in their hands, holding entire ecosystems in the space of five fingers. They'd studied the encyclopedia pictures; they knew that even as they held them, the tiny bodies were changing into something else.

Later, they returned with jars, lids poked through with nail holes for ventilation.

'Shhhhh, Luce, there's a frog. I'm gonna get him.'

They stood still, frozen. Then Levi's hand shot down like lightning, grabbed the frog and put it in the jar. He put the lid on and submerged the jar in the ditch for a few seconds to let some water in.

'What do you think frogs need to live?' he asked her.

'I dunno. Some bugs, I guess. Flies and mosquitoes and things. Are the holes big enough for bugs?'

That night, after making sure the holes were the right size, Levi left the frog outside on the front porch. In the morning, the jar was lying open on its side and the frog was gone.

'Hey, Luce, come here. Look, the frog's gone. Did you let him out?'

'No ... it was probably a magic frog. Maybe it said some special frog spells, like "Open sesame, oogledy boogledy bee, now this captured frog is free."'

She walked away humming to herself. He watched her back for a while, not sure if she was telling the truth.

∽

March 25, 1983

(House) Wren,

It's mating season. The wrens are quite vocal, constantly communicating back and forth. Today I heard a couple of them singing a duet. The call of one alternated with the call of the other in such exact succession that they sounded like a single bird.

Winter Wren: *Troglodytes troglodytes*. Frequents mossy tangles, brush piles, ravines, roots along stream banks. Song, a rapid succession of high tinkling warbles and trills, long and sustained.

House Wren: *Troglodytes aëdon*. A wren of the orchards, farm-yards. A stuttering, gurgling song, rising in a musical burst, then falling at the end.

I see how Levi is lost without Lucy and Lucy is lost without Levi. Normal for twins, I guess.

As long as they're both in or around the house, within shouting distance of each other, they're fine. But when one is gone, at a friend's house, away on a field trip, wherever, the other one drifts around like a ghost from room to room, through the trees and grass, with a vague look, disconsolate.

And there are fights, followed by silences. Lucy will provoke Levi, doing something to pull at him, irritate him, anything to see a ripple on his calm exterior. But he won't react, at least not in the way she wants. Instead, he withdraws into stony silence, ignoring her, making her pester him even further. It's as if he won't let himself get angry with her, so instead he starves her, removing himself, until she breaks, apologizes, and they call a truce.

I wonder if they know how good our lives are out here, in these fields and trees. How lucky we are to live in this place, protected from the mad beat of the world.

I wonder if they know how much I love them. How much you love them, through me. Your presence just a part of who I am now. The man with the woman inside.

Levi walks for hours during these autumn days and nights, learning the streets of the city. Here, everyone dresses in black, protecting their soft places. They are savvy, fashionable, always colour-coordinated. They walk quickly, cigarette smoke trailing behind them. Colours make a statement – here I am, they say, notice me – while black is the colour of invisibility. Levi finds himself wearing black, too. Joining the flow. He understands. A smile could threaten our safety. Could break us open. Stay cool. Just keep walking.

He takes the subway every chance he gets. It's soothing down in the dark caverns with the regular stops and starts, the hum of the cars along the tracks, the driver's voice announcing stations, marking progress up and down the line.

Sometimes he rides the trains for hours, from one end to the other. It's good when he's working on a problem in his head: what to build next, which materials to use. He watches the sparks fly up and reflect off the inside of the tunnels as metal pushes against metal. The monotony of the ride, the soothing flow of passengers – these things clear his mind, teach him what he needs to know. Down under the city he finds the space that brings him answers.

Levi used to collect insects. He would crouch low, pause, scuttle quickly, waving his invisible antennae, sensing sensing sensing. The bugs never suspected as he quietly approached. Before they knew what had happened, they'd be in a jar, peacefully, without any harm to their delicate structures. He and Lucy would feed them and see how long they'd live in captivity. They liked seeing the perfectly rounded bites caterpillars took from the leaves on twigs they propped up inside the jars. The caterpillars would climb the twigs to the underside of the lid, where they stayed, that much closer to the sun, that much closer to freedom. Lucy kept hoping that one would live long enough to spin a cocoon and turn itself into a butterfly before her eyes. It never happened, though. Whenever she found a dead monarch she would put in a cedar box that their father made for her. She called it her magic box.

When they were small, their favourite time was the hour before sleeping when they would clamber into their beds and their father would read to them. The night would fill with the smell of the printed pages, the sound of his voice, the spine crackling as he flattened the book in his big hands.

On weekends he would take them to the library. They would each pick a story for every night of the week. Fourteen books altogether, more if they were short ones, and still more for their own individual reading. He told them about how their mom loved books. 'She used to work here, not that long ago,' he would say in a soft voice, looking over their heads into the distance.

At night when Lucy and Levi lay in the dark, they pretended that she was there, glowing white and true on the edge of the bed. They would drift off to sleep untroubled, imagining her fingers in their hair, soothing them to sleep while she whispered stories into the air.

Levi passes the same man each day when he walks down St Laurent. He sits smoking cigarettes on a crate between two buildings, wrapped in a blanket. He wears a wool beret with a beaded brooch pinned on it, and sketches with pastels onto pieces of cardboard. It's obvious to Levi that he's not crazy, that he's an artist who uses the street as his studio. Levi imagines that he has an apartment in one of the buildings he sits between. He must like coming down there every day, watching the people pass by, thinking and making up stories, spinning out visions in his head. Pigment is pressed deep into the skin of his hands, his eyes are violently blue. Levi wonders what he does with all those drawings. Does he give them away, or is there a wall or a room somewhere, a field of colour composed of seamlessly joined squares and rectangles, the fruits of his days? Each time Levi passes the sitting artist, he feels a thrill of recognition run through his core.

When he was sick as a boy, Levi would lie in bed and stare up at the ceiling. His eyes would become unfocused and he would see the space machine, a rocket that lived on the inside of his right eyelid, its tail flaring, shooting out of the earth's atmosphere. He would follow it as it zoomed from one spot on the ceiling to another, connecting the dots with a smoking trail of fire. He can still see the rocket when his eyes are closed. He follows it with curiosity, allowing it to guide him to new places.

In Montreal, Levi draws and writes in a coil-bound sketchbook that he carries in his backpack wherever he goes. Collecting fragments that capture his imagination.

Daydream: A man who wears the sun on his head.
(Possible imagery for the sculptures?)

He stands inside a pyramid. Cool and dark. Light slivers slanting through the half-open doorway. Outside, unbearably hot afternoon. Cold inside him like inside this golden building. He stands alone, legs pillars of stone, chest wide and impenetrable, skin deep brown from sun and heredity.

Jump forward in time.

He has married the woman he loves, a queen already, in stature and spirit, before he made her one by law. She knows the secrets of plants and oils. When she puts her hands on him, his chest opens wide – she unlocks him and he spills out. Each morning he washes his face in rose water that she makes herself. He was half-formed before her; she added her spittle to his dust, making him a man.

∻

July 6, 1984

Wren,

I guess it had to happen sooner or later.

The other night I looked in on the kids before going to bed. I turned on the hall light and from the doorway I could see that Lucy was already asleep in her bed with her back towards me. Levi was still awake under the blankets, making furtive, up-and-down movements that I recognized only too well. When he realized I was there, he stopped and quickly began adjusting the bedding as if his life depended on it.

'Just coming in to say goodnight.' I turned away, sounding as nonchalant as possible.

'Goodnight.' His voice muffled.

'See you in the morning.'

I proposed the idea of separate bedrooms the next day at dinner.

'Not that there's anything wrong with sharing a room. But wouldn't it be nice to have a little more space?'

They looked dubious.

'It's just an idea. Why don't you think about it for a few days?'

Levi came to me later when I was in my study. He seemed nervous and pensive.

'I've been thinking about it, Dad, and I'd like to have my own bedroom.'

Just like that, as if it were his idea. As if I hadn't mentioned it earlier.

'Okay, Levi. Sure. Which room would you like?'

'The spare room beside our room. The green room. Lucy wants to keep the room we have now.'

He was shifting his feet around a lot as he spoke.

'Fine.' I closed my book. 'Why don't we go upstairs and I can help you set it up right away?'

I suppose it will take them some time to adjust, but I think it's the right thing to do at their age.

Levi needs a model, so he calls a number from a bulletin board at school.

When she rings his doorbell and he sees her standing there, he recognizes her from drawing class. She looks Japanese. Her hair is long and straight, the blackest, shiniest black. He had noticed her before, but she seemed aloof. He has enough of his own work to do without taking the time to break someone else's code. Long fingers brush her hair behind one ear. She is wearing a black leather jacket and tattered jeans. Paint-speckled boots. No jewellery.

'I'm Alex.' She reaches out her hand.

'Levi. Hello.' Her hand is fine and smooth, like a swallow.

'Should we go get a coffee?'

Unexpectedly, he hears himself answer yes and reaches for his coat.

They go to a hole-in-the-wall restaurant that she knows, just a few blocks from his apartment. As they talk, Levi begins to feel electric, like all the places where his body meets the air are sparking.

The front sections of her hair are gathered up into a knot on the top of her head, held in place with a thick pink elastic. She isn't wearing any makeup. He notices the barely perceptible movement of her pulse at the front of her neck where her leather jacket is open. She has long elegant hands. He imagines them covered in paint.

'I've seen you in drawing class. Are you a fine arts major?'

'No, creative writing. I'm minoring in art. I do performance art. In French, English and German.'

'Wow, a true polyglot. I'm still a struggling uniglot.'

'You're not as inarticulate as all that.'

He raises his eyebrows and looks out the window beside them.

'No, really I am. Why do you think I'm in fine arts? Words pin things down. With images, you're free.'

'Yeah, I guess it's easier to be abstract with visual art. That's harder with language.'

Levi returns his gaze to her. His green eyes glitter as he speaks.

'I experience it when I'm making things. It's as if temporal reality moves back a step, and I have this extra space to play with.'

'And what do you like to play with?'

She leans back, swinging her legs under the table. Her foot hits Levi's shin.

'Sorry.'

'It's okay. Was that a rhetorical question?'

'No, a real one.'

'Well, I'm making papier mâché animals, but I want to make a life-sized plaster cast of a woman. That's why I called you.'

'And that's why I came to meet you. One of my favourite things is being covered in plaster by cute boys. What's one of your favourite things?'

A slow smile moves across Levi's face. He leans back in his chair.

'As it happens, I like to wrap attractive women in plaster, so we're in luck.'

'I suspected as much.' Her foot hits Levi's leg again.

'You seem restless. Should we walk?'

She slips on her jacket. 'Yes. Let's go.'

They take a rough path up the mountain, cutting steeply through trees and underbrush. The air smells of decaying leaves with a hint of frost. Branches grab at them as they scramble over rocks. She is ahead of him, fast and nimble, like she knows the way.

At the top they stand looking out over the St Lawrence River and the green copper rooftops of the city. They're both a bit winded and warm from the climb. Levi wipes his forehead with the back of his hand and asks Alex where she's from.

'I was adopted, but I've lived here since I was a baby. You?'

'Dad lives on an island in Lake Ontario. I didn't know my mother. She died giving birth to my sister and me.'

'You're twins?'

'Yeah.'

'Do you miss her?'

'Who?'

'Your mom.'

'I don't know. Can you miss something you've never had?'

Alex glances at him sideways, her eyes narrowing.

'Yes, I think you can.'

∞

May 12, 1985

Wren,

Today on the boat, George told me about a time when he worked a fishing vessel off the West Coast. He said there were nights when the water would go bright with sea life. Bacteria and fish eggs would get churned up as the boat passed by, and the wake would be lit with a bluish-white light. Bioluminescence, he said. The same as fireflies.

I've just looked it up and it's true. It's also called 'milky sea phenomenon'. Mariners sailing in the Indian and Western Arabian seas describe moving through waters glowing with soft white light stretching unbroken towards the horizon. I don't know why, but that image has taken hold of my imagination and won't let go. Something about the light against all that darkness of water ...

It's peaceful here now. The kids upstairs. The warm glow of the lamp on my desk. Moths clinging to the window screen. *Lepidoptera*. What are they hoping for?

Did you know that butterflies have taste receptacles on their front legs for savouring flowers?

Whippoorwill: *Caprimulgus vociferus*. *Whip-poor-weel*, repeating in endless succession on summer evenings. Flits away like a large brown moth.

Snowy owl: *Nyctea scandiaca*. Large and white with a round head. Moth-like, noiseless flight.

Papillon de nuit.

The first few flakes of winter snow drift down outside the window, and steam from the sewer grates rises into a cloudy sky. Inside, the choral strains of Palestrina soar above the drone of the heaters. The air is filled with the smell of electric heat mixed with coffee and plaster. Alex is lying on her back on the kitchen table, covered with a white sheet to keep her clothes clean while Levi works above her. He has been careful, taking his time to preserve the distinctive outline of her bone structure. Now he hums along with the chorus of voices as he eases the dried plaster mould off her face.

Free of her mask, Alex opens her eyes and stretches her mouth, flexing her jaw.

'Ah. Much better.' She swings her legs over the edge of the table and sits up. Levi hands her a wet washcloth and she wipes her face, holding the cloth against her skin for a minute, breathing in the warmth.

'Coffee?' he asks her.

'Yes, please.' Her voice muffled.

He brings the mug over and as she takes it her other hand closes around his wrist, pulling him towards her. Their faces are close together. She still has bits of plaster and petroleum jelly in her hair near her temples. Her eyes are steady. He can feel her breath on his face.

'Don't worry. I'm not going to kiss you. I know your heart belongs to someone else.'

She releases him with a smile and cups her coffee with both hands.

He moves away from her and sits on the floor with his back against the wall, not speaking, smoking a cigarette.

She takes a couple of sips of coffee before dressing and putting on her coat, wrapping a rainbow-coloured scarf three times around her neck.

Levi stands up and hands her some money. 'Will you come back next week? I'd like to do some more plaster work.'

She takes the money and looks at him, her head cocked to one side. 'Yeah, I'll come back. If you call me.'

She pulls on her boots and leaves, trotting down the marble stairs, the door banging behind her. Beside Levi, the air where she was seems suddenly empty.

He writes the phrases down in his sketchbook when he finds them.

> *My corpse is permanent, it will not perish nor be destroyed in this land for ever.*
> – Egyptian Book of the Dead

In the morning when he leaves for school, he finds a bright red flaming heart spray-painted onto the sidewalk in front of the apartment. He is sure it wasn't there yesterday. Seeing it gives him a feeling of happiness. He likes living in a city where mysteries can simply appear during the night.

∞

February 5, 1986

Wren,

I was thinking about it when I was coming home on the boat after playing cards over at Ted and Margaret's, and I'm still thinking about it. What they said. The questions.

'What about moving back to the city, Daniel?' Ted asked. 'It might do the twins some good to get off the island now that they're getting older. Widen their horizons.'

Maggie was siding with him. I felt like I was being ambushed. I didn't answer. Just kept looking into my beer, trying to hold onto my composure.

'And what about you?' Maggie asked. 'You must miss having a bigger social circle sometimes. I know how much you loved Wren, but I have a friend you might like –'

'No.' I cut her off. I could hear the harshness in my voice even as I said it, but it was too late. I took a sip of beer and tried to smile.

'Listen, you two, I appreciate what you're trying to do, but things are just fine the way they are. Though it may not look like it to you, the kids and I have a really good life. Better than most people. When Wren was pregnant we talked about all this, how we wanted to get away from the city and give our kids a different kind of upbringing. I'm committed to doing that.'

They didn't press me after that. We found other things to talk about. Though I still find being around Maggie difficult at times. Her physical resemblance to you, and the unmistakable mannerisms – the way she moves her hands when she talks, her eyes squinting when she concentrates. It brings to life the dull ache behind my ribs that I sometimes think I've left behind.

And there was this afternoon, too. Running into Marjorie Flynn in the coffee shop while the kids were at their lessons, her asking me about Levi and Lucy. If I ever worry about them getting a balanced 'family experience' without a woman in the house, what with our family 'keeping to ourselves the way we do.' What does she know about us? Such a damn nosy woman, always looking for something to gossip about.

All the same, I wonder if they have a point. The twins seem happy to me. Can island life possibly be worse than the stink and rush of the city? I still think they can experience all that later, when they decide for themselves that it's what they want.

❧

October 29, 1989

Dear Levi,

Frost has come to the island. The orange and red leaves are crisping up under its grip at night. I've been keeping an eye on your weather – snow already, though I suppose it isn't sticking yet.

I understand why you couldn't come home for Thanksgiving with all your school work, but if you ever need a break, any time, just come. Of course, it would be strange for you here without Lucy, I know. Still no word from her. I've thought about looking for her so many times, but since you were young, I always tried to instill that strength of spirit in you both, so that you would know your own hearts and minds. Now I see that you do. It's so difficult, not to look or worry, but I'm sure you know that. We just have to trust that she knows what she needs.

If you ever need me, Levi, for any reason, I'm here.

Love, Dad

Levi lifts the letter to his face and smells it.

Nothing. Just paper.

When Levi enters the underground, the tepid air gusts into his nostrils, and he feels his past dislocate slightly, as if it were a stencil, laid loosely over his body, that could be moved at will. He is entering the world of minutes travelled between stops, the roar and hiss of locomotion, the labyrinth of tunnels. He buys a cup of coffee and gives himself over to the echoing music of buskers, rushing crowds of passengers, graffiti.

The sounds of the doors gliding open and closed are soothing, and the warm, caraway-seed smell of the air down here lulls him into a pleasant state. He imagines all the connected tunnels filled with water and boats instead of subway cars. Someday he'll go to Venice and float through a webbed world of water. He likes the idea of a moist, dim, timeless city where you can travel endlessly and go nowhere.

Sometimes between stations, the lights flicker and go out for a few seconds. Levi wonders how many times a year desperate people jump in front of the moving trains. What the driver goes through after the muffled thud of the body.

He thinks about the bandaged female forms that are filling up his living room. The stops fly by, prayer beads on a flashing string of darkness and light, mantras flowing out of the speakers at regular intervals: Saint-Laurent, Place-des-Arts, McGill, Peel, Guy-Concordia, Atwater. He thinks of his father, the way he moves people across the water and the freedom it affords him. The evenness of his voice, reading the stories that still play themselves out in Levi's mind.

He gets off the subway before his stop and makes his way home through the side streets. It is Hallowe'en night and the sun has fallen past the horizon. Jack-o-lanterns are appearing in windows and on the winding stairs of walk-ups. A few small ghosts and goblins are creeping out onto the streets accompanied by adults who wait patiently on sidewalks. There is the occasional sound of a firecracker going off, the crunch of dry leaves under his feet, a hint of woodsmoke in the air. And the indefinable smell of snow somewhere behind it all.

He thinks of the times – or was it only once, multiplied in his head? – that they rode through the snow. His body warm from the sun of late afternoon sinking into the navy blue of his winter coat and snowpants, and the heat of Lucy's body behind him on the sled. They had just been to the stand of balsams out past the barn to cut the Christmas tree. Cinders bounded ahead, her chain collar clinking as she snuffled through the snow, then doubled back to join them. Levi watched the silhouette of his father's body as he pulled the sled and the tree forwards, marvelling at his strength. He could smell the sticky drops of sap on his mitts. Lucy was mumbling something about hot chocolate in a sleepy, singsong voice. Levi was memorizing the outline of the trees against the sky.

He is casting the front of Alex's body. He applies the plaster bandages to her legs and hips. Her genital area is protected by a layer of plastic. The rest of her is covered in petroleum jelly to stop the plaster from sticking. Her arms lie in an X across her chest. In the flat space between her belly button and her pubic bone she has a tattoo of a sacred heart, exquisitely rendered in pink, crimson, gold, tangerine and royal blue. Levi's fingers graze the coloured skin. He quickly draws them back.

'Sorry. I didn't mean to – it's quite striking.'

'That's okay.'

'What does it mean? I mean, to you.'

'It was a present I gave myself. To remind me that there's nothing to be gained from a heart that's cold.'

Levi is smiling.

'You don't happen to know anything about one bright red sacred heart that appeared in front of my building last week, do you?'

She looks straight into his eyes with a serious face.

'I really couldn't say. But how extraordinary that they seem to be following you around.'

Levi receives a card from his father with a cheque for two hundred dollars in it and a note: *To buy yourself some more art supplies … love, Dad*. He has enclosed a photo of Lucy and Levi from years ago. They must have been about ten years old, their hair bleached almost white from the summer sun, their father standing behind them with his arms around each of their shoulders, his wavy red hair past his ears and unkempt. They're all smiling widely. Levi can't remember who took the photo – maybe Aunt Margaret or Uncle Ted, or maybe his dad set the timer. He looks at the colour of his own hair; it has darkened a lot since then. So had Lucy's, the last time he saw her.

> *Gone am I*
> *Caught by the Underworld*
> *Yet cleansed and alive in the Beyond.*
> – Egyptian Book of the Dead

ॐ

July 18, 1987

Wren,

God knows how much I love the twins. But if I didn't have these regular hours of reading, and writing to you, I don't know what I'd do.

Trying to finish a book a week, if I can. Logging them for proof. Your words still echoing in my head: 'There's no excuse not to be well-read. You don't need to go to school forever to be a smarty-pants.'

Your wide smile. The smooth skin around your eyes.

And so I maintain our connection, following the trail of words, and leaving this written trail for you.

The three of us don't read stories together any more; it's become a solitary pursuit.

Evening. Windows open. Light leaking from the house out into the black night beyond. The soft bodies of moths flickering against the screens. Chirrup of crickets. Occasional sound of a page turning, swallowing from a glass of water, whir of brains spinning through imaginary worlds.

When I kiss Lucy goodnight on the forehead and ask her if she's going to sleep soon, she says, 'Just one more chapter, Dad.' Tonight she looked up and asked me if you left any jewellery that she could have. I went and got the gold signet ring you used to wear on your baby finger. She put it on and asked me if she could keep it. I told her I was sure you would have wanted her to have it.

I leave them, Levi reading next door to her, trusting them to sleep when they're tired. I have no desire to be the kind of parent who constricts with meaningless rules. I want them to grow up with faith in their own judgement, understanding the consequences of their actions. If you don't sleep, you're tired the next day. It's pretty simple.

I believe that we're a happy family.

An older man wearing a turban enters the subway car, his arms filled with individually wrapped roses. He sits in the seat across from Levi, who has his eyes closed, rocking with the movement of the train. Before long, the smell of the flowers fills the air. Levi opens his eyes. The man nods his head at him, and Levi nods back. When it is time for him to get off, Levi pushes a five-dollar bill into the man's hand and receives a rose the colour of wet blood.

Levi hears her before he sees her. Alex's voice is bouncing off the walls of the metro station, rising up over the escalator and into his head. He follows it, and when he gets closer he hears her chanting, repeating two words over and over:

super heroes super heroes super heroes

When he rounds the corner at the bottom of the escalator, he sees her. She is doing a handstand between a man and a woman who are facing each other, making an arch over her body with their raised arms, holding her legs steady at the same time. Her voice rises up from the subway platform, surprisingly strong in the enclosed space:

> *can lift buildings with a single hand*
> *can make themselves invisible*
> *can swing through the air with no place to land*
> *are truly indivisible*
> *super heroes super heroes*
> *that's what we are*

Levi laughs and applauds, spawning a few weak claps nearby that are drowned out by the roar of an approaching train. He hugs Alex hello and she introduces him to her friends, Frances and Tyler.

'We were just finishing up,' Alex says. 'Do you want to join us for a drink?'

They end up at the Luba Lounge. Blue smoke swirls around them.

'So, these two are my partners in crime.' Alex is beaming as she gazes at them, a glow on her skin. The rose is lying on the table beside her.

'What do you guys do together apart from entertain commuters?' Levi asks. 'Do you ever perform in clubs or theatres?'

Frances lights a cigarette before leaning forward and answering.

'Nope. We don't think people should always have to pay to see performances. It's a bit of an experiment – for ourselves, to just be publicly visible, and for our audience, to be exposed to our brand of poetry, or whatever you call it, without having to pay?'

'How do you keep your morale up?'

'What morale?' Tyler laughs.

Frances adds, 'It's an exercise in ego hardening. You must know this, being an artist yourself. If you let people's opinions get under your skin, you can end up quitting. There's always going to be someone who thinks you're boring, who doesn't appreciate what you're doing, or whatever.'

Tyler is nodding. 'I've grown an invisible armadillo shell that I can activate at will.'

Alex leans back in her chair. 'But, thank goodness, for those moments when extraordinary courage is required, there's always Bombay Sapphire Gin.' Her voice trails off as her eyes rest on the blue bottle behind the bar.

Frances grimaces. 'Gin always tastes like water that's had fermented pine trees sitting in it.'

'It's the juniper,' Levi says, 'That's how they flavour it. I've been researching botanical oils and resins for my sculptures. The oil from juniper berries is supposed to be good for removing toxic material from the body.'

'So, if you get drunk on gin, you'll wake up a new person the next morning, hangover and all, right?' Frances asks.

Levi leans back in his chair. 'That's it. Brand new. Resurrected and shining forth like the sun.'

Tyler is squinting at the bottle over the bar. 'It does sort of look like it has mysterious clarifying properties. It doesn't look mind-muddying at all.'

Alex lifts her glass in a toast. 'Most poisons don't, my sweets.'

Alex and Levi walk slowly, arm in arm, through a light fall of snow that floats in the air around them. It's not too cold yet, and the streets are alive with people and music. An irresistible aroma of sautéed garlic reaches out from a restaurant and pulls them inside, where they eat ginger beef and get drunk on red wine.

Later, in Levi's bed, they kiss like worms, rubbing their faces together blindly, speaking through their skin. When Levi's breathing gets raspy, he has to pull away to use his inhaler. It takes a minute before the medication kicks in. The building next door whirs and steams. He lies back down on the bed and listens, trying to decipher the sound of his breathing as it gets swallowed by the larger respiration of the building.

'What does it feel like?' Alex asks him.

'Like an elephant is sitting on my chest, and I have to use every ounce of energy to focus on sneaking underneath it, into my belly, where there's room.'

'It sounds like drowning.'

'I guess. It's like every bit of oxygen is gradually being used up by someone else, while the air gets thicker and thicker.'

'And your puffer takes all of that away?'

'Like magic.'

Alex turns on her side, places her hand on his chest, her fingers spread wide. The room smells of semen. Like fresh grass trapped in a jar, warm and pungent.

'Levi?'

'Yeah?'

'I'm thinking about doing some travelling. Maybe tracking down my birth parents. Going to Asia and exploring my family history a bit. I wanted to tell you, because if I leave, it might be suddenly.'

He looks at her, the contrast between her dark hair and her skin.

'It's okay. I'm always sort of expecting you to disappear into smoke anyway.'

Alex sighs. 'Well,' she says, 'I wouldn't want to disappoint you.'

'Impossible.' He laughs, stretching his arms up over his head. 'My tolerance for disappointment has already been exhausted.'

Lucy always claimed that his sweat smelled like soap. She'd say, 'I smell more masculine than you do.' Well, this is one time she would be wrong. Tonight he has the indisputable aroma of a man.

Near the shore of the frozen lake the ice was transparent. Beneath it, fish hovered in the dim green light, their slow motion movements imperceptible to the eye. The ferry route was a long black snake of water, covered by large chunks of broken ice, which curved its way across to the other side of the lake. A mile away from the ferry path was a straight stretch of cleared ice that the islanders used as a road.

Lucy and Levi would climb into the cab of the truck beside their father and start out, a few inches of frozen water all that separated them from certain death by freezing or drowning, whichever came first. In winter the lake had its own vocabulary of creaks and groans, expanding and contracting like a sleeping monster, threatening to crack awake at any moment.

After the ferry had passed, the ice pieces would float back across the channel, forming a false surface. Each year at least one snowmobiler would get caught in a squall, misjudge the width of the ferry channel, slip in and drown. Most often, though, they glided safely across to the other side, like walking on water.

> *Her mouth was full of the breath of life.*
> *Her talismans vanquish the pains of sickness*
> *and her words make to live again*
> *the throats of those who are dead.*
> – Egyptian Book of the Dead

Alex and Levi are on the mountain, sitting on a bench in the snow. Their faces are turned to the sun, dark winter jackets absorbing heat. Alex has her head in Levi's lap. Her eyes are closed and he's taken off his gloves to hide his fingers in her hair, which is spread out across his legs.

'Lucy and I used to play Rapunzel Rapunzel in an abandoned cement silo in the back field,' he tells her.

'Did she have the requisite long blonde hair?' Alex asks.

'Yeah, long and tangled. *Fine as spun gold.* She would climb up the inside of the silo and sing, while I pretended to be the king's son riding by below, who is so charmed by her voice that he wants to join her. She undid her braids and pretended to let them fall to the ground, throwing a rope down as if it were hair. Then I climbed up and we balanced there, clasping each other in a really melodramatic way.'

He pauses, the memory unfolding.

'Sometimes we played out the rest of the story, too, the parts where the evil witch chops off Rapunzel's hair and the king's son is blinded by thorns, only to have his vision restored by Rapunzel's tears. Lucy would stare at the sun without blinking to make her eyes water.'

He stops talking. Listens to the sparrows and chickadees in the branches overhead. Alex lies against him without moving.

'Is that who you're in love with?' she asks him.

Levi takes his hands out of her hair and crosses his arms over his chest. There is a long silence before he answers. When he does, his voice is quiet.

'My sister disappeared a few weeks ago. All she left my dad and me was a note saying not to look for her. That she'd be back when she was ready.'

Alex sits up and looks at him. 'I'm sorry, Levi. I didn't know. Do you have any idea where she might be?'

He looks down at his lap, warm where Alex's head was. 'None. She doesn't want to be found.'

⌗

August 27, 1989

Wren,

Something is wrong with Lucy.

When she was younger, she would dance in circles, singing her made up songs. Socks down around her ankles, hair flying in every direction, her impish way of laughing. Looking like she knew things we didn't, singing nonsense until she had no voice left, creeping around the house whispering her spells. I would call her Little Witch.

Now she seems different. Quiet and nervous in some way that doesn't suit her.

I wish you were here. You could talk to her. I try, but I don't know what to say. She smiles a little and tells me not to worry. Then turns back inside herself, holding privacy tight like a cape around her body.

⌗

Alex lies face down on the table. Levi wets the bandage in warm water to moisten the plaster and places it carefully along the line of her spine. When the back cast has hardened he removes it in sections. Then he gets her to turn over and starts on her front, her hands folded across her breasts. These movements have become quite familiar to both of them. Palestrina plays in the background, the choral voices an important part of the ritual.

After Alex has showered and left, he begins to reconstruct her body shape, joining together the casts with more layers of bandages.

He works until the natural light runs out. Then he continues by candlelight, preferring it to the harsh white glow of his work lights. His eyes are partially closed, trusting his hands to find their way around curves, mending the severed halves. By the time he is finished, her body lies complete on the floor, hollow, holding space.

Once his dad explained his job to him. He spoke in a calm, even voice. The only thing that ever gave any hint of a possible fire under the surface was his messy red hair.

'Working on the ferry is a great thing, Levi. All day long my thoughts are my own. I can think, dream, spin stories in my head. I hear the seagulls around me. I smell the breeze off the water. I am my own man. I see people through all their comings and goings, back and forth over the lake. I give them safe passage. Don't ever let anyone tell you it takes a dull-witted man to work a job like mine. It's a smart man who knows how to work for a living and not lose his soul. Remember that.'

As a child, Levi would sometimes go up on the bridge of the ferry at night. It was pitch black except for the dim glow of the radar. He would stand there, breathing in the stale smoke smell, gloved by darkness, watching the cabin lights as they reflected off the gloom of the water's impenetrable surface.

When he was fifteen, Levi's father got him a job working on the ferry during the summer. They woke up at the same time every morning and ate a breakfast of toast and eggs before driving to the dock. Levi would watch as his father raised and lowered the ramp and directed vehicles. He knew everyone who lived on the island, though lately there were increasing numbers of strangers and vacationers.

Everyone liked Daniel, his calm quiet ways. His big hands floating through the air as he waved people into position. *Hello,*

Frank. Good morning, Shirley. Just fine, thank you, and yourself? And then, Levi's hands, as he continued to guide them, father and son, working in tandem. *Keep going, keep going. Just a bit further. Okay, that's it. Stop.*

Once all the cars were aboard and the ramp was back in position, the boat pulled away from the dock and Levi started to collect the money and ferry tickets. Occasionally he overheard people talking in their cars, thinking he was out of earshot. *A fine-looking boy. Good-looking like his mom. Bless her soul.*

∽

September 1, 1989

Wren,

I came downstairs to find Levi's face as crumpled as the piece of paper in his hands.

> *Dad and Levi,*
>
> *I know you won't understand but I'm leaving early. I can't start at the Conservatory this fall. There are other places I have to go, things I have to do. It's nothing you did. I just need to get away for a while. Please don't come looking for me – I'll be back when I'm ready.*
>
> *You know how much I love you both.*
>
> *Lucy*

And now she's gone. Just like that.

Fathomless.

I need your help.

∽

Alex's apartment is a few blocks west of Levi's, closer to the university. He walks down Aylmer Street, past the music building, through the sounds of a man singing opera, a clarinet, a piano, everything mixing together like a Kurt Weill song. Being joined by the occasional bird, the drone of passing cars, his feet crunching against the snow. He stops and looks up at the blue roof and the warm fiery bricks. This is where she lives, beside the music.

Levi knocks. There is a smiling wooden skeleton hanging on her front door. Levi thinks it looks Mexican, probably some Day of the Dead thing. When she opens the door, he walks into a carnival of colours. The warm, golden walls of the hallway open out into a forest-green living room. They continue through to the kitchen, which is robin's egg blue with pink trim. 'Wow,' Levi comments.

She shrugs her shoulders and smiles. 'I'm a failed minimalist. I tried once, but it only depressed me. Life is no fun if you can't pick up something at the flea market because it will clash with your white walls and curtains. *Ce n'est pas pour moi.*'

She moves to the counter, pouring steaming water into a flowered china teapot. The window beside her is open a crack and a tattered typewriter ribbon riddled with words and twisted around the window latch catches in the breeze. She sets the teapot down on the table beside a bowl of fruit.

Levi picks up an orange and starts to peel it. 'So?'

She raises her eyebrows.

'So. It tastes better with chocolate,' she says, pulling a bar out of the big front pocket of her overalls and peeling back the gold foil.

She pours them each a cup of tea.

'What kind is it? It smells weird.'

She grins. 'It's custom-made for inducing creative visions. Good for you artistic types.'

Levi looks at her doubtfully.

'Don't be a stick in the mud. Life is bigger than a bento box. Besides, when was the last time you hallucinated? Like the good Kierkegaard said, "To dare is to lose one's footing temporarily, to not dare is to lose one's life."'

Alex stands up. 'I'm going to get changed,' she says, taking her cup into the bedroom with her. 'Don't go anywhere without me,' she calls out over her shoulder.

Levi sips, looking around him, alternating the earthy, not entirely unpleasant flavour of the tea with triangles of chocolate.

Levi can hear her in the next room, opening and closing drawers.

After a while, she emerges dressed in a rainbow of wool – thick leotards, a knee-length skirt, layers of sweaters – and pulls at Levi's hand for him to join her. He finishes his tea in a gulp, stands up, and sweeps his arm in front of her in a lavish bow. 'Yes, madam. Shall we go out and lose our footing then?'

They're walking down Prince Arthur towards St Louis Square, and the mushroom tea is starting to kick in. It's a sunny day, unseasonably warm, and the dripping sound of melting snow is all around them.

'Look at these rooftops,' she whispers in his ear before jumping on the edge of the fountain at the centre of the park. 'Which one do you like best?'

He watches her. She's making slow, exaggerated dance movements as she balances on the cement. He jumps up behind her and imitates her. Nearby, some dreadlocked teenagers are playing hand drums. People are out walking their dogs. There are bottles of wine being passed around and the smell of dope is in the air.

'I like the one you like the best,' he tells her, balancing on one foot. 'It's the turret, right?'

Now she's turning in circles, her boots tap-tapping on the fountain edge. Her long hair is a shining cape flooding out from the central point of her head. She is a glossy parasol, a black aster.

'Yes. The turret. Home of the prince and princess, eternal lovers, joined at birth, in royal blood, in royal matrimony. Perfectly united for all time.'

Levi glances quickly at her but she's not looking at him. She wasn't talking about him. She was just talking.

'Want to hear a story, something that happened here?' she asks him.

He follows her gaze up to the cloudy, curved window on the top floor.

'Only if it's true.'

'Of course it's true. One hundred percent.' She sits down cross-legged on the edge of the fountain. Levi sits down beside her.

'It's dark. The blue, glowing dark before dawn. Imagine a young queen, indeed, still a princess, gazing out from the turret. Her blood as blue as the sky. And she is pregnant.

'Her lover has just ridden off, a prince himself, the hooves of his horse clattering against the cobblestones. Her skin is still warm with him. Yet, alas, the man she loves is not the man she is to marry. This is the tragedy of her life. And so, the two have been planning their escape.

'After a long day of waiting, when the sky has darkened again, the prince returns to the princess, concealing in his vest a strong potion in a small bottle.

'In her fragrant bed, the lovers share the liquid, feel their limbs go soft against each other, and close their eyes. Wrapped in white sheets, the three of them, prince, princess and unborn child, become bluebirds. Rising up, they appear first as pale smoke, and then, growing wings, they move towards the window and out, brilliant against the darker sky. Their human bodies abandoned on the bed, white and cooling in the night.'

Levi is staring past her, his jaw tensed.

'What is it?'

'Nothing.' He looks down at his hands.

'What? Tell me.'

'Nothing – it's just that – Lucy and I used to play these games. Where I would be the king and she would be the queen. I just ...' His voice trails off. He is shaking his head.

She sighs and puts her arm around his shoulders.

'Sorry. I forgot. Anyway, my little story is finished. *Tout fini.*' She takes his hand and pulls him up.

'And now, sir, let us tarry here no longer. We have many adventures to seek, and miles to go before we sleep.'

∞

September 13, 1989

Wren,

Tell me what went wrong. Did I neglect an aspect of parenting that could have prevented this? Was I too distant, withdrawn? Paying more attention to books than my own children?

My chest hurts. When I go to bed at night. When I wake in the morning. A sort of constriction that has come out of nowhere, my ribs too tight for what they contain.

If only she would phone or write to say she's okay. I called the Conservatory in Toronto just to be sure. She's not there. How can she be silent, knowing how hard it would be for me, for Levi? I didn't see this coming. Somehow I have failed to understand. Failed to see. Failed.

∞

Alex has talked Levi into exhibiting his work. She knows some people with a gallery on St Denis and has helped set up the whole thing. He will have a small one-man show in February. He will fill a room with his sculptures and the city's inhabitants will come to see them.

To prepare properly, he has rented a separate studio in old Montreal. It's a subway ride and bit of a walk, but it's cheap. He relishes the livid bluish-green of the walls, the thick wooden banisters, the musty smell in the old hallways. The prospect of the show inspires him to work harder. The space is filling up with female forms, all of them based on Alex's body. Some of them lie flat on the floor, some are propped up against walls. Some have smooth plaster surfaces, others are wrapped in layers of linen, softer to the touch, absorbent. They all have their hands folded across their chests.

Levi writes on pieces of linen: letters, bits of poems, lines that fly into his head like leaves pushed against a fence by the wind. When the ink dries, he crumples the linen into balls and soaks them in a solution of almond oil with essences of cedar and benzoin.

Wringing them out, he pushes the linen balls into the emptiness of the plaster bodies. He adds another layer of plaster and punctuates it with minerals. Turquoise at the throat. Silver for the liver. Carnelian for the sex. He fills the eye sockets with pieces of quartz, to add light to the face and lapis, for clear vision and the gift of prophecy. He paints a series of papier mâché bracelets the creamy yellowed colour of old ivory, embellishes them with gold leaf, and stacks them fifteen deep on the forearms.

When the last layers of plaster are dry, he sands the bodies smooth by hand and wipes the dust off with a damp cloth. Using a small brush and a jar of India ink, he paints tiny figures onto the plaster. Frogs. Trees. Snakes. A bird. A beetle where the heart would be.

There are also canisters, ranging in height from one to three feet. He begins with large glass jars, building up their surfaces using a blend of papier mâché and plaster until their shapes are strange and irregular. He embeds patterns of stones into the plaster as it dries, turning the jars into glittering archeologies. He makes lids shaped as indefinite animals, hybrids that are part insect, part reptile, part mammal. Then he covers them in paint that he rubs off before it dries completely, making them appear worn, historic.

He writes more words on linen: *les reins, l'estomac, l'intestin, les poumons, le foie, la vésicule biliaire*. After soaking the linen pieces in a syrupy mixture of ebony gum water and cassia, he wrings them into balls and puts each one in a canister. Ensuring the preservation of the organs.

He folds other pieces of soaked linen into small squares, tying each one with string. He hides these aromatic parcels in the soft sculptures – the mummies – nesting them between the layers of linen wrapped around the limbs.

A final step: the anointing.

Unguent:
  6 cups almond oil
  60 drops essential oil of rose
  40 drops essential oil of chamomile
  30 drops essential oil of sandalwood
  30 drops essential oil of myrrh
  20 drops essential oil of cinnamon
  10 drops essential oil of vetiver
  1 cup wheat germ oil

He pours the mixture into his hands and starts rubbing it into the soft sculptures, turning them from white to amber. The room fills with a rich warm smell, sweet with an earthy base note. Floral essences combined with gummy resins. His hands tingle, becoming deep pink as the oils bring blood to the surface of his skin. It takes him about an hour to fully coat one body. There is no reason to rush. He takes his time and makes it good.

Somewhere around three or four am, having spent hours completing the latest phase of work on a group of sculptures, Levi stands up and stretches. His body tired in the good way of having worked hard, he sprinkles powdered incense onto a charcoal burner and lights it, wreathing the room with smoke. He uses the finished canisters to mark the perimeter of each sculpture, like sentries. Satisfied for the moment, he crouches and sits on his heels. He rocks slowly forward and back, the richness of the oils and incense permeating his clothes, hair and skin. He sits this way, in the dark with the bodies, for a long time.

Maybe it's straining to do his work in this dim winter light, but Levi's vision has been failing. He has ordered some glasses. Crazy, big ones with heavy black frames, but he likes them.

∞

November 15, 1989

Wren,

Down at the beach this afternoon I found a turtle shell. Empty, against the strata of the rocks. Disappeared from its home.

The tree branch we used to swing off is now in the water, bent low from the years. The old yellow rope, frayed and forgotten. Sand on the shore, constantly shifting. Pieces of quartz moved into new positions by the waves to repeat the endless process of grinding down. Eroding away to nothing.

Tonight, reading one of their old books, stories by the brothers Grimm. Remembering how blonde their hair was. How they glowed sometimes with a light that didn't seem entirely earthly.

Just now, glancing outside at the trees, I thought I saw a naked body suspended in the upper branches, lit up by the moon. Of course it was a play of light, a trick of the eye. Though for the briefest moment I wasn't entirely sure. (Was it my own inner deadman? Was it you?)

I am hollow from all this missing. Like the bones of a bird. Filled with space instead of marrow.

Indigo Bunting: *Passerina cyanea*. Deep, rich blue all over.

Snow Bunting: *Plectrophenax nivalis nivalis*. High clear *teer* or *tew*. Musical purring note and a rough *bzzt*. Travel in flocks, look almost entirely white drifting over a field. Like snowflakes.

Ten years old. They were playing house and Lucy was the mother. She wore her long green velvet Christmas dress to make her more grown-up. They lay on top of her bed like parents are supposed to, pressed together, their arms around each other. And then there arose an awkwardness in the air between them, something because of the closeness, the feeling of their bodies like that. Lucy stood up abruptly and walked towards the imaginary kitchen.

'Dear husband, what shall I make us for dinner?'

Levi sat up and smiled at her.

'Why don't we have my favourite, salmon? Here, I'll help you.'

They bent over the invisible counter, pretending to fillet the fish like they'd seen their father do, and pouring wine into the air. They drank a toast and sipped delicately. The moment had passed. It wasn't the sort of thing you talked about.

'You look a little vague around the edges. Can I shave you?'

Levi reaches up and runs his hand over the three days' worth of stubble on his face.

'Sure, if you want to.'

'Good. It'll give you your outline back.'

He sits on the toilet seat in her bathroom with his knees spread apart. Alex stands in the V his legs make, lathering his face with jasmine soap. Levi can see half of himself reflected in the bathroom mirror when she moves to one side, a clear track appearing down his cheek and neck in the razor's wake. Her breath is warm and smells faintly garlicky. Above the mirror, there's a long strip of paper taped to the wall with INSURGENCE written on it in black paint.

'I've never shaved a face before.'

'You could use a bit more pressure.'

'I don't want to cut you.'

'You won't.'

She moves slowly and carefully, until the rasping sound of metal against hair gives way to the smoothness of skin. She knocks the razor against the edge of the sink, where it leaves a scattering of pale brown whiskers. Levi rinses and dries his face, then lets Alex rub moisturizer into his skin.

'You smell good,' she says.

'I smell like you.'

The curtain of multicoloured plastic beads swirls and catches the light as she laughs and pulls Levi by the hand through her bedroom door and onto the bed. She straddles him, with one arm on either side of his head, bringing her face down close.

'Now, can I dress you up?'

'I appear to be already dressed.'

'No, as a woman, silly. I'll dress up like the man instead.'

'Why?'

She laughs again.

'Because it's fun? Because it's good to try the shoe on the other foot? Because I think you'd make a pretty girl?'

Levi considers, his gaze moving past Alex's head, up towards the ceiling.

'You don't have anything that will fit me.'

She jumps up and starts pulling clothes out of her closet, laying them out on the bed.

'This will work. Here, put this on.'

She hands him a skirt made of a crimson stretchy material that he has never seen her wear. She undoes his pants, pulls them off, and shimmies the skirt up over his legs and hips. It clings rather becomingly. She whistles at him, handing him a pair of black stockings and a turtleneck.

'You can be my beatnik babe, okay? And I'll be your man on the road.'

She helps him put his hair back in a wide black headband and they line each other's eyes with kohl. Alex tells him to stay still while she applies mascara, eyeshadow and lipstick.

She pulls her own hair back into a tight bun close to the nape of her neck and puts on a navy wool toque. Wearing jeans and a black t-shirt, she looks nondescript, but doesn't exude much manliness. She is still a beautiful, fine-boned woman, and he is still six feet tall with broader shoulders than her. But for a few hours, they play the parts. They smoke cigarettes and drink wine in her apartment while she spouts Ginsberg and Whitman. Finally, he lets her have her way with him.

'I celebrate myself, and sing myself,' she says, smiling drunkenly, her hair falling down around her face. 'What I assume, you shall assume.'

Outside, the snow falls, turning all the green rooftops of Montreal to white, bright powder.

November 30, 1989

Wren,

Frost in the air.

The house desolate without the twins.

I miss you.

I take care of things here: working, filling the birdfeeders, hanging suet in the trees for the blue jays, feeding the cats. When it's cold at night they curl up beside me on the bed, one near my side, one near my feet, purring. Small consolations grown large.

And so I carry out a routine.

But how my body still longs for yours. How I miss the warm enclosing of you around me, the easy sinking into the centre of you.

Levi wrote me a letter asking me why I don't date. If I want to but just don't let myself.

The thing is, I never got past being madly in love with you.

They say the initial romance wears off, that day-to-day life settles in and the other person loses their shine. You see their flaws and the spark disappears. They say that, but it never happened for us. After being married for five years, together for seven. There was never anyone else after I met you. There can never be anyone else.

If I didn't know that my heart was beating in the barrel of my chest, I'd say that it had left me when you died and that you hold it now. Until my work here is done and I can come to where you are, and stay.

They're at Alex's. Levi researching an essay, Alex at the computer, working on the promotion for Levi's show. She has been designing posters, planning ads for art magazines. She says she wants to do it, that she likes it, has the energy for it, so Levi lets her, relieved. He doesn't have time for any of that. He's too busy building the bodies.

He flips through a book about Joseph Beuys. He stops at a photograph called 'Show Your Wound.' The book is from the library, but he rips the page out anyway and tucks it in his bag.

He makes life-sized papier mâché models of hearts. Hearts as they would appear unhinged from the body. Veins severed, still, like a picture in a dictionary. When they dry, he paints them with silver and gold iridescent paint. Each one fits perfectly in the palm of his hand. A fruit, a frog, a carefully preserved organ. When the time is right, he will make a cavity in the chest of each sculpture, where he will install a pair of hearts joined as one. Because he can. Because he's an artist.

There were evenings when his father would come home from work and go straight into his study. He always needed a lot of time by himself. The smell of smoke from his pipe would slip out from the crack under the closed door. Levi and Lucy would have to fend for themselves. They didn't mind.

Lucy would put on an old apron of their mother's and make sandwiches. Towering sandwiches with salami, lettuce, thick slices of cheese and lots of pickles; everything she could find in the fridge. She would boil eggs and make mugs of instant coffee that they drank with milk and lots of sugar. When the feast was ready, they would arrange it on a tray, along with salt and pepper, paper napkins and ketchup, and take it upstairs to one of their beds. They would pretend they were stranded at sea on a boat, where they would eat and read aloud to each other until they were rescued.

Their father would eventually emerge from his room, hair dishevelled, looking tired. He'd find them, floating on the bed with their emergency candles lit, surrounded by open books, bread crusts, egg shells.

'What time is it, kids? Are you hungry?'

'We've eaten, Dad. Look, we saved you some.' Lucy would offer him whatever was leftover from the plates.

'Did you eat enough?' he would ask, returning their smiles and nods, before biting into a crust of bread or part of a pickle and wandering off downstairs. They would hear him in the kitchen, clattering dishes and listening to jazz turned up loud on the stereo. Then they would resume their game until he reappeared at the top of the stairs and announced that it was time for a story, and then off to bed.

There is one group of sculptures that is like shadows: thin and spectral, blackened with paint and resins, the embodiment of negative space. Levi groups them together in corners, their dark bodies anchoring one another, creating vacuums he must step widely around to avoid. He calls these the Illusions; they are doomed to spend eternity in the underworld. As draining as they are, Levi finds he needs them in the room. They provide a sort of familiar balance. The pull of that cavernous space.

Levi's sketchbook bulges wide with paint- and water-wrinkled pages, glued scraps of paper, photos. He writes questions to himself:

What are you doing?
I'm making artificial hearts.
Why?
Because all head and no heart makes life a dull journey.

What are you doing?
I'm giving form to the thing that has no form.
What are you doing?
I'm exorcising.
What are you doing?
I'm making you look, ask this question, give consideration to these
thoughts.

In the myth, the body of Osiris was rent into pieces and strewn across the land.

(In order to assemble, one must first disassemble; one must go to pieces.)

Yet, the question remains, what if Isis had not sought out the pieces of his scattered body?

What if, after grieving his atrocious end, she had left well enough alone, and gotten on with her life?

He records dreams there, too. Daydreams and night dreams. The one about the greenhouse:

Lying on my back, surrounded by thick air, a feeling of being closed in. A greenhouse, full of humid plant breath. Too warm. Through heavy-lidded eyes, I see Lucy coming towards me. We're both wearing white cotton underpants. She lies down on top of me, her arms curling under my shoulders, her mouth beside my neck. We say nothing. I close my eyes, holding her as close as I can. And then, there is air, space, where she used to be. I am holding nothing; it is as if my body has absorbed her. I feel terror slide into me, a thin, cold sheet of metal. I am alone.

∽

December 3, 1989

Wren,

I found something in the woodshed today: *Archilochus colubris*, the smallest of all birds. One of the kids', forgotten. A flat Birks box lined with white tissue paper. A pair of ruby-throated humming-birds, lying beak to beak. A long time since they sipped nectar, their tiny bodies rather badly decomposed. Tucked in beside them, this poem (I think in Lucy's handwriting, though I can't be sure):

> *Be Like the Bird*
>> *Be like the bird, who*
>> *Halting in his flight*
>> *On limb too slight*
>> *Feels it give way beneath him*
>> *Yet sings,*
>> *Knowing he hath wings.*
>>> *– Victor Hugo*

December 10, 1989

Dear Levi,

Well, winter has finally descended here. There, too, I guess.

After work, I've been spending some of my evenings looking at seed catalogues, figuring out what to put in the garden next year. Looking at the bright colours of flowers and vegetables at this time of year makes it seem less cold and dark.

How are your studies going? Your sculptures sound very interesting, to say the least. How did you arrive at the idea of mummies? Be sure to keep me posted about the date for your show – I wouldn't miss it for anything.

In response to your question about me dating again, I have to say I've never really had the desire since I lost your mother. It may be hard for you to understand, but she was unlike any other woman. No one has sparked my interest since her. I suspect I may be the type of person who only loves like that once in a lifetime.

And of course I get lonely sometimes, but who in the world doesn't?

Don't worry about me, Levi. Look after yourself and make your art. Life is best when it's simple.

Love, Dad

P.S. Let me know when you think you'll be home for Christmas. Maybe Lucy will be back by then. We'll make it work somehow.

It has been snowing again. Outside the studio window, the sky is lit up golden-white, reflecting the city off a low ceiling of cloud. The streets below turn to soft brown sugar as pedestrians navigate the snowy sidewalks in their boots and mitts, steaming breath hanging suspended in the air for a few seconds like word balloons before disappearing.

Levi and Alex are finished their work for the evening. He has made his last cast of her body, and she sits wrapped in a blanket beside the heater.

Levi is at the hotplate, boiling the kettle for coffee, when he feels her behind him, her arms around his waist. He turns and kisses her, the blanket gone, her skin warm, her body slight under his hands. She pulls him over to the work table.

'Wait,' he says, his voice low. 'Do you have any lipstick with you?'

She reaches down to the floor for her knapsack and hands him the tube. He carefully applies a thick layer to her lips, bleeding the colour over the edges so that they look fuller, overdone. Then he does the same to her nipples, applying the lipstick in circular motions, piling the colour on, making her aureoles large, a dark reddish-brown, broad and bitten.

He whispers in her ear. 'Now you do me.'

She kisses him, pressing the colour onto his lips. Then she takes the lipstick and fills them in, making them as red as her own. When she moves down to his nipples, he's undoing his pants. She barely has him coloured in before he has positioned himself against the table and lifts her up on top of him. With one hand, he moves his finger across her mouth, dragging the pigment over to her cheek.

The kettle is boiling in the corner, fogging up the windows. Snow is falling. When he's inside her, barely moving but deep, she closes her eyes and he feels her shudder. He lets himself go then, the tips of her long hair brushing his legs. They hold each other in the steamy air, their winter-white bodies smeared red. Warm and luminous from the game.

Before they fall asleep, Alex speaks softly into Levi's ear. 'I've got another story for you. It's called "The Jeweller."'

'A woman lives in a land where there are turquoise trees. As you can imagine, the people who live in this place have different sorts of jobs than we do here. This woman's job is to grow diamonds in her body from pressure that builds up underneath her skin. Every so often, she goes to a doctor and gets her growths surgically removed. The doctor washes the blood off each shiny rock, holds it up to the light, and places it on a clean white cloth. The medical community continues to marvel at her ability to create riches in her tissue.

'After the operations, she deposits her riches at the bank. She has become a very wealthy woman. In answer to those who question her vocation, she smiles and says, "Why make cancer when you can make diamonds?"'

'She has a bowl full of them at home beside her bed. She likes to rake her fingers back and forth, listening to the sound of their gentle clinking against the glass.'

∝

December 12, 1989

Wren,

There is the brief span of time when I wake up in the morning before I remember who I am. A few seconds of suspension. And then this life closes down around me. I remember myself, the circumstances of fate that have made me their owner. You and the children gone. What I have is my job, my books. These words I scribble to you. The world that exists in my head.

I'm here alone.

The mistletoe branches I cut are in a jar on the table. I arranged them with an eye for symmetry, as you would have.

I wonder, who is a person if no one is there to receive him?

Does he really exist at all?

∝

Levi is making large wooden sarcophagi for his queens, as he's been calling them. Preparations for the future life. Inside each box, he leaves all the provisions each queen will need to keep her from wandering outside the tomb in search of food. Wine for her thirst. Dates and almonds for her hunger. A mask with which to disguise herself. A dress to keep her warm. A statue of a god to answer all her questions. The likeness of a small bird to relay messages back and forth between worlds.

His sketchbook is rich with the smell of resins and paints. He writes on a page stained the colour of tea:

> *The body of Osiris was closed in a tamarisk tree until Isis could find it and bring him to life again.*
>
> *Isis became a divine mourner, toiling ceaselessly for the recovery of her husband's sacred body.*

> *Questions:*
> *Who are you who comes?*
> I AM A MAGICIAN.
> *Are you complete?*
> I AM COMPLETE.
> *Are you equipped?*
> I AM EQUIPPED.
> *Have you healed the limbs?*
> I HAVE HEALED THE LIMBS.

He pretends that Lucy is here with him. He tells her how he went to the art gallery in Toronto and the Henry Moore sculptures reminded him of dinosaur bones. He heard a woman say they were 'colossal junk.' He whispers about things that go beyond words. The finest pencil line to suggest a world. His own shadowy place between dream and awake. He can see her. The sun is shining on her face, in her hair. She is tossing her head back, laughing. With her small features, she looks fragile. He wants to put his arm around her, to protect her.

Instead, he writes words on pieces of linen and hides them inside sculptures. He assembles her bones, he pulls together her limbs. He will carry her heart to her, returning it to its proper place in her chest. He will bring her back, so she is here, embodied and intact.

III

Ceremonies Concerning the Right and Left Arms

PHINEAS AND LUCY ARE ON THE UPPER DECK of the ferry. The day is atypical for December – sunny and clear, cold without the insulating layer of clouds. Lucy has found a sheltered corner out of the wind for sitting in, for turning her face to the sun and closing her eyes. Phineas is inside the passenger cabin reading.

They have an agreement.

Phineas asked her if she was ready to see herself. She said yes. He said he knew a way, but that it wasn't easy, and she would have to trust him.

'Haven't I been trusting you all along?' she said.

So now they are on this journey.

When she asked him where they were going, he replied, 'To the woods.'

'Which woods?'

'The woods of your childhood. Metaphorically, of course,' he answered with a smile.

A tremor ran through her body. 'What will I do there? It's the middle of winter?'

'Just exist. Without props or costumes.'

'Can I read?'

'No.'

'Write?'

'No. You can sit. Lie down. Rest, maybe walk a little, but always with your campsite in view. All you have to do is stay put and contend with what presents itself. I'm pretty sure you'll find enough to occupy you within fifty feet of your tent.'

She told him he was making her nervous. He looked into her eyes, his face soft, his voice sounding tired.

'It's okay, Lucy. I'm on your side.'

Before she agreed to come he asked her a few questions.

'Did you consider having an abortion?'

'No, somehow it never entered my mind. Getting rid of it like that?'

'And the not eating – did you ever think that it might harm the baby?'

'No – I don't know – it wasn't deliberate. I wasn't thinking in a straight line. I just couldn't eat the way I used to.'

'And when was the last time you cried?'

She pauses.

'I don't remember.'

∽

Lucy sets up her tent on a carpet of pine needles in a small clearing surrounded by ferns. She brought all the things on the list Phineas gave her: sleeping bag and blanket, two tarps, inflatable mattress, small propane stove, flashlight, extra batteries, a few candles and some matches, warm clothes, rain jacket, boots, lots of bottled water, a small pot and a mug.

When they arrived it was late afternoon, and Phineas went to set up his camp somewhere away from hers, he didn't say where. Then he came back and helped her gather a pile of branches and twigs that they found lying on the forest floor.

'It'll probably be pretty wet and cold during the next few days. If you keep this under a tarp, you'll have dry wood for starting fires. Do you know how to start a fire?'

He showed her, watching while she tried.

Now she sits next to the orange flames, a mug of hot tea in her hands. Some concoction Phineas brought that smells like old socks. She grimaced when she first tasted it.

'Not exactly Earl Grey.'

'You'll get used to it,' he said. 'It starts to taste good after a while.'

The fire crackles, catching when Phineas flings the plant he's been rubbing back and forth between his palms on it. The air smells like wood smoke, burning sage leaves and damp cedar.

'So what happens now?' Lucy asks.

Phineas sits down on a log on the other side of the fire.

'You'll eat nothing for three days, maybe four, depending on how you manage. You'll consume only water and the tea mixture that I'll leave here for you, as much as you want. You're already underweight, so to fast for longer than that would be dangerous. We aren't going to speak after the first night. I'll always be nearby, though you won't see me. You'll feel weak and you may experience strange dreams or visions. Try not to worry if this happens. If there is an emergency, call out for me and I'll come. All right?'

She swallows. 'Okay.' Her voice sounds small.

He stands up to leave. 'See you in a few days.'

Lucy watches his back as he disappears into the shadows of the trees. The fire is a tiny oasis of light, poor protection against the darkness that is building around her. There is a familiar feeling in her stomach that she doesn't have a name for but knows is not hunger.

On edge, she barely sleeps. So many noises, owls that sound like ghosts, strange rustlings and scratchings. Finally, when the first bird starts to sing and the sky begins to lighten, she is able to sink into a fitful sleep, only to be wakened a couple of hours later by the scolding of chipmunks outside her tent. She gets up, makes herself a cup of tea, and here she is.

I seem to have slipped down the rabbit hole.

Lucy sits on a fallen log and surveys her surroundings. Tall trees in a circle around the clearing. How quiet it is down here on the spongy moss floor of the forest. Only the sound of birds and wind in the trees. Sounds then silence, repeating. Sunlight flickering in and out from behind branches, into her face, her eyes.

She imagines the clearing to be full of wood sprites, sylphs and elfin spirits, slight and shimmering. A hint of small laughter. If she sits very still, maybe they will approach. Dancing creatures of the air, touching down. Nothing like wild animals. Like bears or wolves or cougars. Creatures that would certainly break sticks on the forest floor as they approached, crashing out of the undergrowth to carry her off.

She pours herself more tea and wanders around the clearing. She finds an old hollow cedar tree, a secret cave to push her back up against. Inside, through the cool dimness, she sees tiny bones down in the corner near her foot. Some small animal that came here to die. If she encloses her body in this tree, maybe she will die, too, and come back to life as someone else, someone new. She holds her face over the steam and sips. Wonders what the tea has in it. She closes her eyes and pretends she has a wall to write on. Imagines the smooth feeling of the pen as it makes contact.

Element:
*   a great force of nature*
*   basic or essential*

a primary, integral part
one's accustomed or preferred surroundings

She lies on the fragrant layer of pine needles that cover the forest floor and looks up at the sky through the tree canopy. Moss beards hang down from branches all around her. Her body relaxes into the ground, tired from endless movement, the effort required to make itself smaller, fitting more into less. She is too heavy to move, weighed down by the fatigue of flapping her wings like some kind of hummingbird.

Dusk gives way to darkness. Trying in vain to fall asleep, Lucy is haunted by images of the woman in the box, living in her world of dreams, wasting away behind glass. The woman floating, sleeping, not touching the world. Her perfect white skin, her small, preserved body, her refusal to age. Lucy knows she will die soon if she stays in her box much longer. She may look like she's alive, her chest may rise and fall, but she must be dead inside. Young, alone, sleeping beauty forever.

It starts to rain sometime during the night. Lucy wakes up, chest heaving, hot, broken into a sweat. There are tears on her face, running down into her hair. She tosses and turns, unable to sleep as rain hammers mercilessly against the tarp above her tent. Unable to hide from the voice in her head that is getting louder, ruining her peace. *What am I doing in this forest? What am I doing out here in the middle of nowhere?*

She thinks of Dorothy and the glittering red shoes. Begins chanting the words softly to herself: *There's no place like home, there's no place like home* … Until sleep finally claims her.

In the morning, shaky in the knees, fleece jacket zipped up to her chin, Lucy makes tea on the stove. She scratches a mark on a stone beside her tent to keep track of time: day two. The rain has stopped, but the birds have gone quiet, hiding themselves away in the places birds do. Lightheaded, she drifts through the trees, moving carefully to avoid the many large brown and yellow slugs that are coming out of hiding, leaving their slick mucilaginous trails.

She leans up against the rough bark of an arbutus tree and touches her hair. As it has grown, she has been twisting it into knotty dreads, black and terrible. She's become a Gorgon, head full of vipers. A Pandora with her frightening box. All the evils inside. Pandora who did a bad thing. Levi's face flashes through her mind. She starts humming loudly, forcefully, pushing the images away. *Art and love have always been my life ... I have never hurt anyone.*

She spends the afternoon lying curled up inside her tent, avoiding the chill of the damp air. Emerging only a couple of times to boil water on the stove. Whether it's the tea or the lack of food, she doesn't know, but her thoughts begin to flow backwards.

Down in the woods beside the house, she had a fort where she used to make thick stews from dirt, water, branches and leaves. She served them on broken bits of dishes she found buried around the tree roots, feeding her dolls as they sat patiently on stumps at the makeshift, knee-high table. With big round lettering, she wrote down the recipes carefully on lined paper: pine needles, rain water, flower petals, maple keys, a dash of pebbles, a sprinkle of moth dust, leave in the sun for one hour to bake. Enjoy. Use as a garnish when available: snake skin, lilac blossoms, dried bug carcasses, feathers from a baby bird.

They would swim for hours beside the smooth, round rocks that covered the shore. The silky green underwater hair of seaweed insinuating itself around ankles. Slimy sludge squeezing up between toes. Scaring themselves with thoughts of sea monsters only feet away, lurking at the bottom of the lake, blind, cold-blooded, hungry for the tender limbs of children.

On the dock, their bathing suits stuck to their skin, drying slowly. Afterwards, hair still wet, towels wrapped around them, scrambling up the incline to the house.

Then, warm in their clothes, the soft inner fleece of sweatshirts and cotton socks. The clean, deep, hard-earned tiredness that comes after a day spent in water and sun. Warm and comfortable, with the whole night ahead of them: a fire outside, stories, and later, the faithful embrace of sleep.

Their father used to call her his little witch with the pointy feet. She was a good witch then.

Now I am the wicked witch, here in the enchanted forest. A witch who murders children. Ruins families. Who is nibbling at my little house? Brother, father, mother? Baby? Where are you? I can't see.

During the night, her sleep is restless, the dream of Levi's face looking down at her being played over and over. Nothing she can do to stop it, to turn back time and make it right.

Early the next morning Lucy is awakened by the sounds of birds. Exhausted, she floats up on the thin mattress beneath her, her eyes suffused with the pale blue nylon glow of the tent. The sun is barely making the sky pink. Hungry. Lost in the woods without a crumb. Cold and alone. She needs arms to hold her, a warm body to comfort her. She needs a clear pathway, a magic potion to fix everything.

Outside the tent, she takes off her pants and stands up to pee, legs apart, like a man. The golden stream starts haltingly and then gains force, steaming into the cool forest air, making a flat sound as it hits the earth and is absorbed. She savours the warm pleasure that rolls through her pelvis.

She used to go in the lake at home. And sometimes in the bathtub with Levi when they were young, she would secretly pee a little, feeling the heat intensify in the water around her vulva, and he would never know.

Lying on her tarp against the forest floor in a tenuous shaft of afternoon sun. The smell of pine needles is crisp and familiar. Christmas. Cutting the tree with her father and Levi. Being pulled on the sled, dragging the tree after them. Cinders joyful in the deep snow, her black body a punctuation mark against the white. Holding onto Levi from behind, her arms around his waist. The world exactly as it should be.

Long before their calamitous flailing against separation. The single moment that would dismember their shared body, flinging the pieces to opposite ends of the country.

There is a series of chirps, a scurrying movement in the undergrowth. She pulls herself up on an elbow to look, her mouth dry, her arms shaking. She knows that chirp. The bird hops out onto a log and cocks its head at her. A wren. She recognizes the small tail that sticks straight up. A friendly wren come to visit. Lucy starts laughing, at first a giggle, then a rolling belly laugh. She laughs until she is doubled over, until her stomach hurts, until tears are rolling down her face, until finally she is lying flat on her back, looking up at the sky. Quiet.

She wakes during the night in a panic. The placenta – what did she do with the placenta? Did she throw it away, flush it? Did it even come out? *Maybe it's still inside me, killing me even now.* No, she saw it come out, she knows she did, shrivelled and ugly, but she saw it. She's heard that some women eat theirs, make a stew with it, but she didn't. Where is it now? Should she have eaten it? *Should I have eaten?*

Daylight. Lucy drags herself to the hollow tree, her back pressed into the certainty of wood. It draws grief out of her body like a magnet. She stays there, crying the tears she has been collecting for months. Using the tree as her lightning rod, sending her excess voltage down into the ground. She lets these things be taken out of her.

The morning after, she smelled different, like she had a piece of fish inside her. Levi's tide of dwindling half-lives, falling back down her channel. The smell of death in a place that sees no light. Everything gone bad. She knew then that her body had betrayed her and it was time to leave the island.

When it slipped out of her, it was half-formed, ugly and beautiful at the same time, slippery like those tadpoles they used to catch that were halfway to being frogs, with big bulging eyes and stunted legs. Tiny monsters. Most of them died before they were full-grown. 'That's the way things work in nature,' their father told them. 'It's called survival of the fittest.'

Her mind floats away from her body, somewhere high above the trees. Out of the silence, she hears it, the voice of the one she carried for those weeks. Communicating as if their necks are bent towards each other, foreheads touching. *I came knowing that my stay would be short, that I would leave one night while you were dreaming. All purposes are served.*

Something in her releases.

She picks a small bouquet of violets from the forest floor. Using her pot as a shovel, she digs a hole near the bottom of a tall tree.

She opens her backpack, takes out the wooden box and unties the cotton scarf. Without opening the box, she places it in the hole, putting the violets on top of the lid. She scoops dirt into the hole with her hands, packing down the earth, piling it up. Tears make her blind, she wipes mucus away from her nose with the back of her hand. She stays there, beside the mound, arms wrapped around herself, rocking back and forth, until she is empty, until all she can do is crawl into the tent and sleep.

She can see herself from above, like in a dream. She is lying on her back in the middle of the clearing, her eyes flickering open and closed, half awake and half asleep. Phineas stands a few feet away from her looking towards the edge of the clearing. There, Lucy sees a ghostly version of herself, white and translucent, hovering among the cedars. She watches as the vaporous form approaches Phineas and extends an arm to him. When the hand touches his lips, Phineas opens his mouth wide and inhales, sucking the fog into his lungs until the air in front of him is empty.

Turning, he walks over to where Lucy is lying and kneels down beside her. He puts his mouth just above her sternum, cups his hands around his mouth, and blows. Taking deep breaths, he continues to exhale forcefully against her chest five or six times. Lucy looks down at herself and sees her eyes start to flicker. Phineas stands up and stretches briefly before turning around and walking off into the trees.

Lucy opens her eyes. Awake but groggy. Phineas comes and puts a lemon with some honey on it up against her mouth. When she tries to bite the lemon, he tells her, 'No, just take juice for now.'

And then, later, he is there again, telling her that she was getting too weak, that it is time to start eating. He spoons warm broth into her mouth, follows it with half-spoonfuls of something like oatmeal.

'I had a dream … a ghost … ' she tries to tell him.

He places a finger against his lips. Tells her to keep resting, that everything is okay now. She slips back, lets sleep fold over her.

When she wakes again, she is more alert. There is a bowl of thimbleberries beside her. She starts eating them, one by one. Her fingers are black-smudged. Her head is next to the open tent door. She smells smoke in her hair. A breeze moves gently across her face and lazily lifts the nylon tent flap back and forth.

Drifting, she imagines a room where she lives and works. Wide windows framed by transparent white curtains. A jar of wildflowers, dropping pollen. Low shelves, painted the green colour of leaves. Blue walls with her lists on them, written in messy dripping colours. She is sitting cross-legged on the floor in front of a door that opens onto a balcony full of plants. Flowers. Blossoms. Summer. The feeling of warm air against skin. Light clothes freeing her body, hovering where they used to insulate. A heaviness lifted. Being able to breathe again. Here she plays piano. Here she sings songs. Here, music fills her days, her nights, her body.

She can hear Phineas making rustling sounds outside the tent. When she lifts the flap back and steps out, he hands her a steaming cup of soup.

'You look good.' He is smiling. 'How do you feel?'

She takes a deep breath and stretches her arms up above her head. 'Different.'

'You've been through a lot. It will probably take a while for you to feel like your old self. When you're finished drinking that, we should head out; we're done here.'

'I had a dream that you ate my ghost,' she tells him. 'Then you puffed on my chest to give it back. Crazy, huh?'

Phineas smiles again. '*Oneiric*. From the Greek *oneiros*, or *dream*.'

On the ferry, gazing out at the lush tops of passing islands, Lucy feels a cramping in her abdomen and a warm surge between her legs. She goes to the bathroom and sees the familiar reddish-brown smudge on her underwear. She finds a quarter in her backpack and buys a pad from the dispenser on the wall. When she pulls up her pants and feels the soft cushion between her legs, it is soothing, like a hand holding her there. She sighs, relieved. She is still intact.

On the way back to her seat, she reaches up to her chest, moving her hand absently back and forth. It isn't there. Somehow she has lost the pendant Phineas gave her. Then an image flashes behind her eyes and she can see it, lying half-buried near a rock by the fire pit that they covered over with pine needles and dirt. St Jude catches some light through the tree branches and winks silver as it returns to the elements.

IV

The Parting of the Waters

LEVI IS IN THE STUDIO finishing one of the sarcophagi when the phone rings. It's his Aunt Margaret.

'I'm sorry, Levi, but there's no easy way to tell you this. Your father died a couple of hours ago.'

When he is silent, she continues.

'It happened when he was at work. The doctors said his heart was enlarged and that he died instantly and probably painlessly. I'm so sorry –'

Levi can hear her crying. He stands holding the phone, frozen.

'I just received a letter from him yesterday,' he says quietly.

'I know, it's so hard to believe. And for you, both parents … ' She blows her nose.

'He said he had been looking at seed catalogues. Making plans for the summer garden.' Levi's voice is flat and unfamiliar as it leaves his mouth.

'I know,' she says. 'This is such a shock.'

She pauses.

'Do you have a way of getting in touch with your sister?'

'No. I still don't know where she is. She hasn't contacted us.'

He clears his throat and grips the phone with white fingers.

'I didn't get a chance to write him back … '

'Levi –'

Through her tears, she tells him she'll call about the funeral arrangements and be in touch again soon. They hang up. Levi stands still, staring out the window, the phone beeping in his hand. Outside, the city is being coated by a slick veneer of freezing rain.

He calls Alex. She comes over and the rain drums against the roof as they make love, hungrily, like they've never touched before. Then, when Levi's eyes are closed and his head is back, the name slips from his mouth.

'Lucy ...'

Too late.

'What?' Alex says, pulling her head from his shoulder to look at him.

He hasn't opened his eyes.

'What did you say?'

He shakes his head. 'Nothing. It was nothing.'

She untangles from him and sits on the edge of the bed.

Levi lies back against the sheets, looks over at the definition of her spine, the fine line of bones that his hands know by heart.

'It was nothing, Alex. Really.'

She twists around quickly and faces him. Her voice is tight. 'You said your sister's name while we were making love, Levi. That is not nothing. I know you miss her, but this is too much.'

She puts on her clothes quickly, stabbing her legs into her pants, pulling on her sweater, grabbing her coat and bag. He stands up and tries to stop her.

'I have to go, Levi. I can't talk about this right now.'

She pushes by without looking at him.

When she is gone, he closes the door and stands naked in the dark.

'My father is dead,' he says into the empty room.

He gets dressed and makes the journey to his studio. Inside, he turns on the lights and surveys his collection of queens. Then, something in him rises up. He takes a two-by-four from his workbench, raises it over his head, and brings it down against one of the sculptures. He does this again, fury racing through his veins, clenching his teeth as the plaster starts to crack and give way. He strikes the body repeatedly until it is in pieces: the stones, the linen spells, the aromatic layers of cloth and plaster reduced to a pile of rubble.

Finally, he stops, exhausted. He stands, sweating, breathing heavily, looking at the ruined sculpture on the floor in front of him. A phrase jangles through his mind, something from his notebook: *In order to assemble, one must first disassemble; one must go to pieces.*

He sinks to his knees and feels himself begin to shake, tears hot on his cheeks, his voice raspy with sobs. A sound he barely recognizes. He curls over onto the floor and lays himself flat against it, gathering plaster dust and pieces of the crumbled sculpture into his arms. With these sweeping motions, with each movement of his body, he calls out to Lucy. Asks her forgiveness. Tells her that he needs her here now.

Somehow, she will get my message, she will hear me. She will come.

During the drive home, Levi stares past the windshield of the rented car as the winter-brown fields flash by under a grey sky. He has a headache. He remembers his Aunt Margaret and Uncle Ted's house in the city. When they visited as children, he and Lucy would play outside in the yard with their cousins, while inside, their Dad talked with Maggie and Ted.

Levi's most vivid memories are of the family alone on the island. Lucy and him in their imaginary landscapes, their father retreating to the containment of his solitude. The times they did visit friends and relatives somehow never seemed as real. Paler, in comparison.

Ted and Margaret's house hasn't changed much since the last time he visited. The wooden bench on the front porch is still here, as is an old basket filled with dried flowers.

He rings the doorbell, his breath frosty, hanging in the air. Nothing. He rings it again. He hears a commotion inside, then the door opens and Margaret appears. She pushes her glasses up towards the bridge of her nose and smiles thinly, drawing him towards her for a hug.

'Come in, Levi. It's good to see you.'

He follows her to the kitchen and sits down at the table. The bare trees in the backyard are dark skeletons against the sky. She pours two mugs of steaming coffee and puts a tin of muffins on the table.

'Help yourself. Raspberry oatmeal.'

He thanks her but doesn't take one. He didn't ever notice as a child, but now he can see the resemblance to the pictures of his mother. The high cheekbones and green eyes, though her hair is a different colour, more strawberry than blonde.

'Still nothing at all from Lucy?' she asks him.

'No.'

'It must be so hard for you. You two were always close.'

'Yeah, I guess.'

'You guess?'

'I mean, yes. But we were planning to leave the island for different schools anyway. And I'm sure she's okay.'

His voice breaks, and he tenses his jaw muscles. Swallowing.

Margaret reaches across the table and takes his hands in hers.

'You know, Levi, you can stay here for a while if you want to. This must be such a lonely time for you.'

He pulls his hands away. Tries to twist his lips into something like a half-smile.

'Thanks. I'll be okay. Other than the funeral, I can't really afford to take time away from school right now. I have a lot of work to do.'

Her eyes are wet as she looks at him.

She stands up and goes to one of the kitchen drawers, pulls out an envelope and passes it to him. A set of keys falls into his hands.

'Your father left everything to you and Lucy. If you want, I can help you go through his things, when you're ready.'

Levi nods and stands up, looking distractedly at the floor.

'Thanks, Aunt Margaret. Sorry – I don't mean to be rude, but I have to go.'

'Levi, listen.' Her voice is soft. 'You don't have to do this by yourself. At least stay here with Ted and me until the funeral.'

He shakes his head. 'I'll stay at the house. I'm sorry. I just really need some time alone.'

He turns and heads towards the door.

On the porch she gives him another hug. Tells him to call if he needs anything. Anything at all. He nods mutely, holding the envelope tightly in his hand. As he walks down the steps he can smell her perfume on his cheek. Roses. He wonders somewhere in the back of his mind if his mother smelled like this.

Levi parks the rented car at the end of the dirt road and walks the mile to the house. Everything still looks the way it did when he left. The old ditches and barbed-wire fences. The fields and trees. It really hasn't been that long. He is enveloped by a sense of the familiar threaded with an anxiety that escalates as he approaches the house. All his cells are letting loose their parachutes of memory. Bubbles of ink, bursting open and seeping in.

They are about seven years old. Playing a game inspired by the book of mythological stories their father is reading to them.

Lucy sets up a chair outside in the long grass near the plum trees. She wets Levi's hair with water from a plastic spray bottle. She cuts a damp lock, curls it around into a smooth O and slides it into a red velvet bag, along with a piece of her own hair.

'You can be the king and I will be the queen, okay? We'll make up magic spells.'

They tie long stems of Queen Anne's lace together for crowns. They dance around in circles, sprinkling maple tree helicopters over each other's heads, chanting. Each of them makes up a line and they repeat it together.

'We are a hundred times blessed! A hundred times blessed!'

'We will live forever and ever! Forever and ever!'

'Our castle is filled with gold! Filled with gold!'

'A million times true! A million times true!'

When they stop, they are out of breath, laughing and dizzy. She puts her hands on his shoulders, holding them both steady. She says, 'In real life, if we are ever apart, we can always say the spells to ourselves, and that will bring us together again. Okay, Levi? So we will always be able to find each other in the whole world, no matter what.'

Levi's feet crunch against the thin layer of snow on the driveway. As he approaches the front porch the cats appear at his ankles from out of nowhere. They weave around his legs, purring loudly, meowing as he leans down to scratch them behind the ears. When he unlocks the front door they bolt into the kitchen towards two empty dishes on the floor. Levi scoops them out some cat food from a bag under the sink. He leaves them there eating voraciously and wanders through the back hallway into the living room.

The door to his father's study creaks open with a slight push. The walls are lined with books. Levi never spent much time in here. It was always his father's private place, inner sanctuary at the end of a day spent outside.

On the desk there is a battered copy of Peterson's *A Field Guide to the Birds* and a black and white photo. His parents are standing on a boat, smiling, their arms around each other, their hair blown back.

It surprises Levi to see how young they look, probably not much older than he is now. Scattered around the room on the bookshelves, there are pictures of Lucy and Levi at different ages. Swimming. Skiing. Holding hands. Together.

The house is shaking with wind and thunderclaps. Levi stands at the door to her room. The window glows white with lightning that seems impossibly close. Lucy lies huddled on her side, her eyes open.

'Luce, are you awake?'

'Yes. Who can sleep through this racket?'

She rolls over to face him. He is standing beside the bed, shivering.

'Can I get in with you for a while?'

'Okay.'

She turns back the sheets and he climbs in. They lie together on their backs, touching along the length of their bodies.

'Are you warmer yet?' she asks.

'A bit.'

A low grumble of thunder builds into a crescendo, making the house shudder, followed immediately by a flash of lightning that seems to burst into the room. They both startle and Lucy pulls the blankets up over their heads. They're laughing, hiding together in their tent, blocking out the storm.

'There's no reason to be scared, Levi. We did the spell that protects us for all time.'

'I know. I'm not scared now.'

The night it happened was later, right before she left the island.

Lucy stands at his door in her thin cotton nightgown. The dim light from the hallway illuminating her around the edges.

'Awake?' she whispers.

'Yeah.'

He moves over and she climbs into the warm spot left by his body. The night is quiet. Only the sound of their breathing in the dark.

'So. We're off soon.'

Her whisper is warm on Levi's cheek. He doesn't answer. He turns towards her and his mouth brushes hers in the smallest kiss. She returns it, resting her lips on his for a second. Then they are opening their mouths to each other, tongue seeking tongue. Levi pulls his head back, catching his breath. He can make out her eyes, wide and staring.

Then their mouths are together again, arms pulling one another tighter.

When he slips inside her, she gasps, and he freezes.

'Does it hurt?'

'Yes ... no.'

He starts to move over her slowly, his breathing deep and raspy, his eyes never leaving her face. He is making low sounds in the back of his throat. She pulls his head down and covers his lips with hers. She pushes her tongue deep into his mouth and his body lets go. His face in her hair, a crying sound, a smell like moss. They hold each other for a long time.

Levi is sitting at the desk, staring blankly out the window at the silhouettes of trees. Dusk has gathered itself around the house. The air is still, filled with the kind of silence possible only in the country. Levi switches on the lamp, casting a golden pool into the dark. He looks down. His elbows rest on a black book with a hard cover. A journal. Looking up at the shelf above the window he sees a long row of similar books. Carefully numbered on the spines.

He opens the volume in front of him. Some dried flowers slip out from between the pages onto the desk. Lily of the valley. They used to grow along the front of the house, sheltered by the cool shadow of the cement verandah. He remembers their strong smell at night.

The last entry his father made was written four days ago. The day before he died. Levi begins to read.

V

How the Shadow Joins to the Body

SNOW IS FALLING. Outside Levi's studio, the city is bright and muffled, glowing from the light reflected off clouds.

He is making the final touches to his sculptures. Handel's *Messiah* is playing on the radio.

He drills a hole in each papier mâché heart and lines them up in pairs, one silver, one gold. Next, he joins each pair of hearts with a length of clear plastic tubing. Using a jig saw, he cuts a square hole in the chest of each queen, and inserts a pair of joined hearts into the cavity. He prepares sheets of cut glass to fit across each opening, so that the hearts will be visible through their windows. Linked but separate. Each one ready for backup in case the other fails.

He falls asleep with Alex's head resting on his chest, her hair falling forwards across his torso. After hearing of his father's death, she forgave him for calling out to Lucy. 'These things happen,' was all she said.

Now, he sleeps and dreams that Alex becomes a flying thing, silken and fine, glittering like tinsel. She floats up out of the bed and through the window. He stands there, watching her flicker against rooftops, her hair floating in slow motion around her head, as though she is underwater. She looks back at him once, winks, and then disappears behind a chimney.

When he wakes up, he is alone. A cold breeze from the crack of the open window moves across his face. The pillow beside him has a shallow dent where Alex's head was. A piece of her long black hair lies stretched out against the fabric. Beside it is a small brown paper bag that has been made into a puppet. Eyes. Nose. A smiling mouth. He reaches inside and his fingers touch something rough and woody. A root: thin, tough, and covered in wiry hairs. He rolls over on his back and places the root in the middle of his chest.

Later, he flips to the place in the journal where his father made his last entry. He uses the pen that he found on his father's desk to write a final blessing for the crossing over.

> *To the good king, my dear father, in his night-bark:*
> *The doors to the windows of heaven are open for you and the*
> *ways of the sunlight are loosened.*
> *May you travel without hindrance, protected and whole for*
> *all eternity.*

∞

The fountain behind the art gallery cascades with diamond water against royal blue and gold-leafed mosaic tiles. Christmas lights from storefronts reflect off the wet city streets. On the corner of Robson and Hornby, a vendor's jewellery stall glitters, a gypsy shimmer of tinkling metal, stone and glass. An older woman is perched under the red umbrella, her brown face deeply wrinkled. She smiles at Lucy, her eyes crinkling up at the corners, her mouth a collection of gaps and a few teeth. Lucy smiles back, her eyes bouncing distractedly between the woman's face and the table.

'A trinket for you, love?' She hands Lucy a ring that she pulls from one of the many bags around her feet behind the cart.

'This one'd suit you real well. Put some colour back in your cheeks, it would.'

Lucy rolls it over in her palm. It is a deep fire-coloured stone, rounded on top, set in yellow metal. Not gold, surely. She slips it on the middle finger of her left hand beside her mother's ring. It fits perfectly.

'Carnelian, love, a wee bit of heat to keep you warm in this damp city.'

'How much?'

She shrugs, laughing soundlessly, watching Lucy with bright blue eyes.

Lucy fishes around in her wallet and comes up with a ragged ten-dollar bill.

'This is all I have.'

The woman takes the money and tucks it into a colourful embroidered purse at her waist. Then she leans forward and grasps both of Lucy's hands in hers, saying, 'Bless you, love,' before releasing her.

On the way home, Lucy stops to buy groceries at an Asian produce store. The woman behind the cash asks her if she knows what the Chinese characters on her shirt say, and Lucy tells her no. The woman says that they mean *dragon*, and dragons are good because they scare away ghosts.

At the apartment, she reads her mail. Bills. Flyers. A free entertainment magazine. She flips through and catches her breath when she sees the small ad. A photo of a sculpture, a dark body lined with coloured stones. Something familiar.

Galerie de Feu proudly presents
Levi Morgan
Le Corps Fantôme/Ghost Body

Solo Exhibition
January 15 – February 15, 1990

Lucy leaves the magazine open on the kitchen table and walks into the bathroom, where she stands in front of the mirror. Taking a pair of scissors, she cuts close to her scalp where the blonde roots have started to grow in, black hair falling in a circle of ashes at her feet. When she finishes, the hair remaining is a fuzzy pale shimmer around her face. Her hands are warm as they drift over her head, fingers touching her eyelids, her mouth, rubbing her lips back and forth, drawing blood to the surface. She gathers up the black hair from the floor and flushes it down the toilet.

Through the open window, she thinks she can smell a berry pie baking, the sugary filling bubbling, spilling over in the oven. She rubs her stomach. She could use some food.

Acknowledgements

With deep gratitude:

To my dearest family for everything; to Jeff Pearce, for generosity, support and being the working artist; to Bronwyn Chambers for stunning cover art and the lifeline of our friendship; to Rudy Candela for his expert lens; and to Leanne Tonkin for her strength.

To those who generously offered feedback on the manuscript as it developed: Howard Akler, Gerry Bratz, Lesley Crowe, Joy Gugeler, Alayna Munce, Ruth Roach Pierson and Bruce and Dale Smith.

For your invaluable support along the way: Hôtel du Parc writing group, Green Room writing group, the gang at Book City, Edna Alford, Kristjana Gunnars, Aritha van Herk, Robert Majzels, Daphne Marlatt, Derek McCormack and Rachel Wyatt.

To everyone at Coach House Books, especially Jason McBride and Darren Wershler-Henry; and to Alana Wilcox, for believing in this book and being a sensitive, superb editor.

To Brad Cran and the Smoking Lung Press chapbook *Hotrods & Grasshoppers* (1999), where an excerpt of *How the Blessed Live* appeared.

To the Banff Centre for the Arts, the Canada Council for the Arts, the Toronto Arts Council and the Ontario Arts Council for essential financial support throughout this project.

About the Author

SUSANNAH M. SMITH was born in Montreal and grew up in Ontario and Alberta. Her short fiction and poetry have appeared in various literary magazines, including *Dandelion, Event, Fireweed* and *The Antigonish Review*. She currently lives in Toronto, where she is writing her second novel.

Typeset in Galliard and Cartier Book Display Italic. Printed and bound at Coach House Printing on bpNichol Lane, 2002.

Edited and designed by Alana Wilcox
Proofread by Mark Truscott
Cover image by Bronwyn Chambers
Author photo by Rudy Candela
Cover design by Darren Wershler-Henry and Alana Wilcox

To read the online version of this and other texts from Coach House Books, visit our website:
www.chbooks.com

To add your name to our e-mailing list, write:
mail@chbooks.com

Call us toll-free:
1 800 367 6360

Coach House Books
401 Huron St. (rear) on bpNichol Lane
Toronto ON
M5S 2G5